North Parish

By

Rohn Federbush

ISBN-13: 978-1494946562
ISBN-10: 1494946564

D066082?

Acknowledgements

The late Barbara Becker encouraged my interest in Ann Arbor's history and enabled my access to the Bentley and Clements libraries which pointed me to Silas Douglas, the first president of the Michigan Historical Society, and the treaty he published and archived in the Ann Arbor District Library.

To my friends, critique partners, and husband, Paul Federbush, of infinite patience and few demands I am eternally grateful.

To Florence Price of My Girl Friday – Virtual Assistant, who urged me to publish the results of my research in this 1818 historical romance as well as the upcoming publication of my 1841 and 1879 novels centered around Ann Arbor's fascinating history I recommend to unpublished authors.

Chapter One

Cheers from the fort's crowd drew sixteen-year-old Dorothy Evans to the river's shore. Two high-ended Algonquin canoes from Lake Erie and a smaller French trapper's canoe advanced toward them on the Detroit River. With each new shout, more yellow aspen leaves tumbled to the ground, crushed under the feet of soldiers and civilians rushing along the riverbank. The sober clothing of the throng clashed with the riotous colors of the maple trees.

A Chippewa runner had arrived the night before to warn, or rather to assemble the fort's population for Bishop Pascal's arrival. Father Sebastian, the Jesuit pastor, rose on his tiptoes to peer down river. Dorothy and her mother stood on either side of the nervous priest. Elizabeth's short, plump figure advertised her success as the rectory's cook. Dorothy considered herself a competent but reluctant cook's helper.

Preparations for meals left little time to think, to read, to dream. She hurried through her daily chores to escape into the priest's extensive library. For more than a hundred years, the Jesuits at Fort Detroit had collected Europe's finest literature. The tomes whetted her appetite for adventure and romance.

As Dorothy waited for the Bishop, histories of Florence, its free thinkers, faces of popes and red-garbed cardinals swam in her head. The band of young and seasoned soldiers from the fort held no interest. They smelled, and treated her as the stuck-up cook's daughter. She was only someone to hand out an extra cookie or two when their buddies weren't around to tease. But in her secret heart, Dorothy was a mysterious spy, an adventurous temptress, a princess waiting to be rescued.

No hint of cardinal reds were in the approaching crafts, only more drab brown and black clothing. Dorothy sighed, breathed in the cool, tannic-scented air and prayed for patience as the ceremonies began. Her chores awaited and her fingers itched to re-open the Italian history she had set aside.

After the first boat emptied its passengers, a sergeant among the troops yelled, "Attention!"

The thirty or so men lined up, tucked in their shirts and squared their shoulders. The newly arrived, tall, mustached officer with soft gray eyes under menacing bushy eyebrows introduced himself to the sloppy, disgraceful bunch. "Lieutenant C. Louis Cass." He returned their salute and marched past them taking time to point out an unbuttoned tunic, dusty boots, or straighten a jauntily placed cap. "Where is your commanding officer?"

"Abed." A young private in the rear yelled without fear of detection.

"This way," Father Sebastian motioned for the Bishop to follow the troops on the half-mile trek back to the fort.

Dorothy's mother gestured for her to follow, but Dorothy shook her head. Elizabeth delayed and tidied her hair until Dorothy relented and drew closer for what she thought would be a reprimand. Her mother merely whispered. "They're going to take more land from the natives. Mark my word."

"Not again. Where will they let them farm now? Is that why the Bishop came?"

"Father says the seven tribes around the Great Lakes will be affected." Elizabeth tucked a loose black strand of hair behind Dorothy's ear. "I guess the Bishop thinks a missionary is needed to persuade the tribes to attend the new treaty powwow."

Dorothy shook her head. "What chance do the natives have to survive, if they disagree?"

"Hurry back to help me." Her mother scurried away to catch up to Father Sebastian.

Dorothy wandered closer to the river. Dark clouds threatened to stop the sunshine's play with the sparkling waves. The second smaller canoe purposefully tread water in order not to be drawn ashore. Dorothy examined its crew. A tall, straight-backed Huron sat in the front of the boat. Behind him a younger native caught her eye. The shifting sunbeams highlighted the man's blond hair. His face seemed lit from within.

His eyes dreamily swept the shoreline past her, then sharply returned as if he had been startled into remembering something. Something important.

Me, Dorothy thought. He's looking at me. For a moment her breath seemed to stop.

She couldn't help rushing forward to mingle among the native men helping the two pull the boat onto the sandy shore. The natives nearly bowed before the tall Huron. He spoke kindly to each. Did he personally know their families? Then he introduced the younger man to them, "My favored son." The older man inclined his head proudly in the direction of the blond young man, whose ethereal bearing evoked the capability of walking on water.

Noticing Dorothy among the group, the older man said, "They call me Ponthe Walker."

Dorothy nodded but could not keep her face turned away from the infinitely more interesting younger man.

"And my adopted son, Perish North."

"I'm...I'm," Dorothy was sure she'd never remember her own name. "Dorothy Evans. My mother is Elizabeth, the rectory cook."

Perish stepped forward. "A pious believer then?"

Dorothy gained full use of her tongue. "More of a favorite doubter of the Lord's. Like Saint Thomas? You know the one who had to put his hand in Jesus' side before he would believe in the resurrection?"

Ponthe seemed to lose interest, but Perish didn't move.

"I've just returned from my vision quest," he said.

Dorothy believed he grew an inch before her eyes. She slipped a glance down to his boots to see if he'd stretched up on his toes. As she brought her gaze up, she noted his waist adornments, his broad shoulders covered in buckskin. His light blue eyes seemed bleached by the sun, or his vision.

"The manhood rite," she said, trying not to check. A stiff breeze lifted her hair, cooling the nervous sweat on her brow.

"You've heard of the Midewiwins?" Perish took a step closer.

Dorothy could smell a scent of juniper. "I have, but aren't you too young?"

Perish laughed.

A thrill passed through her at the clear, rich tones of his voice.

When his father began to lead the natives back to the Fort Detroit, Dorothy boldly pulled at Perish's elbow. "Walk with me."

Perish slowed to stroll beside her.

Dorothy smiled as winningly as she knew how. "Tell me."

"I can only share Orenda's vision message with family." His face was serious but his eyes were friendly.

"Adopt me," Dorothy said, then raced ahead of the group. Aware of her silliness, she knew her mother would be needing help.

* * *

Perish watched the snowy show of petticoats as the dark-headed girl fled toward the stockade. His nostrils flared catching the scent of lilacs.

His father stopped, waiting for Perish to catch up before they continued to the fort. "Her hair is nearly black."

"Brown eyes." Perish pulled on one of his blond braids to anchor himself in a suddenly unknown landscape. "But she wasn't wearing the red-spotted squaw cape."

"But was she the girl in your vision?" Ponthe asked.

"The vision was taller, older." Perish moved his hand above his eye level.

"Could have been floating," Ponthe said. "You haven't shared your vision with Renault or Kdahoi yet?"

"No." Perish was still held in the dream world of the girl's dark eyes. He shook himself to respond in detail to his father. "I wanted to keep my word to meet you at Fort Detroit, before I met with Mother." He laughed in relief at his good fortune. "Then I ran across your runner's path."

"Dorothy Evans might have been less welcoming if she'd seen you when you came into the Bishop's camp."

"True." Perish hadn't washed for a fortnight and his hair had been dank with sweat and grime. "I hadn't considered the Bishop's idea of bathing of much worth, until now."

"Beauty's going to have a heyday with your vision." Ponthe shook his head.

Perish was surprised that even now his father doubted the Great Spirit's way. "It seems you have a bond with Dorothy Evans."

"Can't help liking her courage." Ponthe said. "Not many parishioners under Jesuit rule voice their doubts in public."

"She's still a child." Perish tried to dismiss his attraction to her bright eyes, her pert smile, that dance of energy.

Ponthe said not a word, only nodded.

"Father." Perish stopped walking. His stomach attacked him with a great qualm, "I need to see Kdahoi."

"Of course," Ponthe said. "Your mother will be waiting. Tell Beauty I will meet with her when she comes to the fort. I'll make your excuses here."

Without another word, Perish ran down to the beach and launched his canoe.

* * *

Raisin River Camp

An evil wind seemed destined to slow his trip down to the Raisin River's mouth to his mother's village. The trip was difficult in the canoe meant for river use instead of slicing the storm waves on Lake Erie.

At the Raisin River camp, the moon's position told Perish he'd reached Beauty's isolated wigwam close to midnight. Perish smiled. If need be, he'd be able to find his home blindfolded. He wrapped himself in his blanket outside the entrance and waited for dawn.

"Perish," Beauty scolded in the morning. "I nearly broke my neck falling over your lazy carcass."

Perish had missed her laughter. He bowed as men did to their mothers. "I had a vision."

"I see. First coffee, then symbols."

After his mother's breakfast of corn flapjacks, Perish realized a certain tension had left his body. Across the river the Potawatomi village was coming to life. Dogs were barking and familiar cooking sounds marked the morning. "Why is it I can only relax here?"

"You've been safe here for many years." Beauty said. "The world outside is filled with tales of violence."

"Is it true you told Governor Hull to abandon the fort or you would scalp him yourself?"

"Renault told you that nonsense." Beauty smoothed her plaited hair down, in her habitual show of vanity, the only one Perish could recall.

"My Copper Harbor dream was a peaceful one."

"I'm glad." Beauty cleared away the remnants of their morning meal.

"I stayed in the cleft of rock, where some men leave pictures of their vision guides." Perish recalled his heightened awareness. "A lightning storm from the west rolled past me but I could still see the islands in Lake Superior. I was wet with the rain, hungry, and cold.

Then someone lifted my chin, or I looked up into the pelting rain to the tops of the cliff. A woman in a red-spotted cape drifted on the wind. We were eye-to-eye when she spoke."

"What did she say?" Beauty couldn't hold back her curiosity, but she kept her head bowed away from Perish.

Perish tugged on his mother's buckskin skirt as he had as a child. Still Beauty wouldn't meet his eyes, so he told her. "She asked me how many generations of children we would beget."

"Beget?"

"A Biblical phrase. To give birth." As Perish explained the word, his body remembered his initial visceral response to his dream girl at Copper Harbor, which matched his reaction to Dorothy's appearance at Fort Detroit. Was she the one, his intended mate? He prayed the Lord's will would be accomplished.

"That was all?" Beauty seemed disappointed. Her green eyes were full upon him now.

Perish dug into his memory to find something more for her. "Hmm. I think I fell asleep then. When I woke up the sun was shining and even my clothes had dried. I must have slept through an entire day." Perish stood up and stretched as if refreshed from that long nap. "I have enough energy to run all the way to Fort Detroit."

Beauty insisted he give her more details. "What did she look like? Was she a white-haired, old witch? A young woman? Smiling?"

Perish attended to his bedroll. "I met her at the fort."

Beauty dropped the coffee pot. "Already?"

The campfire sputtered, too.

"I hope so." Perish frowned. What if Dorothy wasn't the same woman as his vision? Where would he start his future if Dorothy wasn't his intended mate? "Her hair was nearly black and her eyes a dark brown."

"A native." Beauty seemed satisfied.

"No." Perish watched his mother sit down too hard. "Her name is Dorothy Evans. Her mother is the Jesuits' cook."

Beauty held her head with both hands. "I know of them. I'll have to meditate on this. I'll make more coffee. Did you bring any tobacco?"

Perish was embarrassed now. "Sorry, Mother." He began to gather the rest of his belongings. "I can barter for some at the fort."

"Don't go on my account. " Beauty flashed angry green eyes at him. "Renault will be here tomorrow."

"Should I wait to tell him about my vision?" Perish decided to stay with his mother until then. He loved the quietness of their home camp. "I could help you get ready for winter."

"Will you be gone?" Beauty seemed worried.

"You've been without me for three winters now." Perish accompanied Ponthe when he tended his fur traps throughout the last few winters. The landscape was safer because fewer white men ventured out in the heavy snows.

"I'm getting older." His mother straightened her back as if a kink had suddenly caused a pain. Not one year of age showed on her face, her eyes were clear, her teeth sound.

"I could bring Dorothy here for you to meet." Perish refused to think of Beauty as an aging woman. "Or, you can visit with her when we join Ponthe at the fort."

A bright smile flickered for a second across his mother's face. "Yes," she said. "We'll wait for Renault to join us."

Beauty retreated into her wigwam and Perish laid down resting his head on his bedroll. "Now that I'm a man, Mother." Perish tried to choose his words carefully but there was no gracious way of asking. "Where do your green eyes come from?"

"A Chinaman," she called from inside the wigwam, and then laughed.

The old answer kept its secrets.

Perish said, "I wish you could have seen Ponthe with President Monroe."

"I know Ponthe was taller." Beauty exited her rounded abode, straightening from her bowed position. She handed Perish a new porcupine-quill vest. "Why do the whites need more land?"

"White men want to carve a new river out of dry land." Perish stood and Beauty placed the vest over his head, helping him tie the side trusses. "Wagons will float farther west for settlers to claim more of our land. "Mother, the vest is beautiful."

Perish picked at one of the beads on his vest.

Beauty slapped at his hand. "Careful you'll undo a whole string."

Perish knew the land-grab story was old, only the excuse was new. "They call the new river they want to build the Erie Canal."

When Ed Renault arrived the next day, his canoe wasn't filled with beaver pelts. Perish remembered Renault's stories of when he first came to the new world as a young trapper, when the land was still thick with beaver. The deer hides and a few fox furs bore witness to Renault's honed and deft trapping skills. In the weeks since he delivered Perish to Copper Harbor, the man had plied his trade well.

At times Perish speculated Renault might be a relative of his mother's, but she denied any family link other than a long affiliation with their French trapper friend.

Renault's hair was streaked with gray. Perish couldn't recollect the gray when they had parted at the slip of the new moon. Had he been so wrapped-up in his own adventure not to notice signs of aging?

"Hard trip, friend?" Perish asked, helping to beach the loaded canoe.

"A bear tried to talk me out of life." Renault drew up his shirt, where the claw marks of the beast still showed red, ugly welts.

Perish forgot his upbringing and drew the big trapper's head down in a manly hug. "I'm glad he changed his mind."

Renault grinned from ear to ear. "Me, too."

"A few salves will erase most." Beauty had caught sight of Renault's raked chest before he could lower his rough blouse. She shook the trapper's hand, a rare occurrence for them.

A glint of moisture shimmered in the old man's eyes before Renault's booming voice told them of other fights with Indians and settlers. The trapper was a peaceful man and Perish chalked up most of the stories to historic bravado in the face of the bear disaster.

Renault finished off another story with a cup of Beauty's coffee, before asking Perish, "So you're a man now?"

"And he's met the woman of his vision." Beauty teased him. "At the fort, a white girl."

"When do we leave?" Renault laughed. "Have to check out a new member of this tribe."

"I'm not sure she was the girl, Mother." Perish could feel a blush rising as his body started to come alive again. Now that he was a man, he'd hoped to control at least this reddening of face.

* * *

Later that week Dorothy's mother was too busy ordering her helpers around the kitchen to be bothered. So, Dorothy was trapped into taking Bishop Pascal and Father Sebastian a decanter of sherry and glasses into the rectory library. She sat the tray down safely, but her curtsy to the Bishop was clumsy. If she had been more graceful, she could have disappeared without them noticing.

"Bella parva," Bishop Pascal said.

"Dorothy, let me introduce you." Father Sebastian pushed her forward. "She has read nearly every book in the library."

"Lovely," the Bishop said. "What do you think of Saint Augustine's conversion?"

"Silly," she said without thinking.

"I beg your pardon," the clerics said together.

Dorothy collected her wits. "St. Augustine based his conversion on his mother's natural worry about his future." The sober pair remained unconvinced. "On a laundry day among the drying linens."

"I don't remember that," Father Sebastian said.

"Never happened," Bishop Pascal declared.

Dorothy nodded believing the whole thing was made up so the saint could paint himself as a devoted sinner in order to relive the deeds. "Don't you think he dwelt on his errors more than he needed to?" It seemed an innocent question to her.

"Of course not." Bishop Pascal was obviously scandalized. "Father, I think you need to review the studies of your pupil more closely."

Father Sebastian scratched the remaining hair on his balding head. "She reads Latin and has read the Old Testament four times, the New Testament eight." He turned to Dorothy a proud smile on his face. "Isn't that true?"

"Yes," she said. "Every morning I wake with a hundred doubts, read all day and put them to rest before I can sleep."

"Doubts?" the Bishop asked in a warning tone.

Undeterred, Dorothy continued. "I think the book of Ecclesiastes says it best when it rightly names belief in a Supreme Being as our vanity's willingness to find the best in ourselves."

"Dorothy!" Father Sebastian seemed embarrassed.

"A lot of work is needed, Father." The Bishop ignored Dorothy so she slipped out into the hall, careful to eavesdrop. "That child could infect a whole nation of natives. Correct her before it's too late."

"She reads everything," Father Sebastian tried to explain.

"Lock this room up and allow her only texts that will illuminate her belief."

"But the Bible?"

"Needs careful interpretation." Bishop Pascal raised his voice to stop further debate. "The laity is ill-equipped."

"I can see that." Father Sebastian acquiesced to his superior. "I'll make sure she is forbidden to enter the room."

Dorothy was devastated. The library was lost to her? Life wouldn't be worth living. Where would her mind go to find solace? Her stomach hurt and angry tears burned her cheeks. She ran to the kitchen. Mother would fix it.

Chapter Two

Fort Detroit

The summer kitchen behind the rectory was aflutter with activity. The women were too busy to notice Dorothy's distress. She grabbed a towel on the way out and dried her tears. In the vegetable garden, Dorothy was surprised to find her mother comparing herbs with an Indian woman.

Her mother motioned for Dorothy to come closer. "Beauty, this is my daughter, Dorothy."

The tall woman turned slowly. Did their meeting hold purpose? Dorothy looked up into her green appraising eyes. "Ma'am," she said.

"I'm Perish's adopted mother."

Dorothy caught her breath. "His eyes are blue."

"You've already met her son?" Dorothy's mother squinted at her, or the sun.

"When the Bishop arrived." Dorothy curtsied to the two women, aware she was in some kind of trouble even here. "Mother," she tried to change the subject to one less stressful to the two women. "Bishop Pascal has forbidden Father Sebastian to allow me into the library."

"Why?" Her mother rolled her apron around her arms. "Did you break the decanter?"

"No." Dorothy used her most injured-innocence tone. "I did mention Ecclesiastes and St. Augustine."

"Mercy, and that would do it." Her mother hugged her. "Never you mind. Those old men can't keep a good mind frozen out of books."

"You like to read?" Beauty asked in a tone warmer than before.

"Dorothy learns everything she can." Her mother let her go, pushing Dorothy's hair behind her ears.

Dorothy smelled an unknown greenery lingering on her mother's toughened hands. "I don't know anything about herbs though."

"Would you like to learn?" Beauty asked. "While the ecclesiastic males forget about your infractions, I could teach you the Midewiwin secrets."

Dorothy's eyebrows rose in surprise. She was impressed with the woman's elocution. "Where is your school?"

"On the Raisin River," Beauty answered. "Elizabeth, do you trust me to take care of your daughter?"

"More than anyone else." Her mother smiled, rubbing her roughened hands together. "Help me entertain the Bishop and she's yours until spring."

"Is that all right with you, Dorothy?" Beauty turned back to Dorothy. "Do you think we could keep you warm and well-fed in my wigwam?"

Dorothy clapped her hands, then kissed her mother's cheek. "Thank you. I need an adventure." Could they tell her nerves were ready to start skipping rope with no rope in sight? Beauty and Elizabeth did frown at each other when Dorothy asked, "Will your son, Perish, be on the Raisin River too?"

"No," Beauty said, adding slowly. "He'll be with his father on the treaty trip." Her green eyes took their time judging Dorothy. "Is that your reason for accepting my invitation?"

"No." Dorothy lied through her smiling teeth. Her insides sank with the threatened disappointment. "You have so many healthful remedies." She knotted up her mother's flapping apron trying to come up with something better to forestall any doubts of her honorable intentions. "Our doctors seem to be fascinated with knives."

The two women joined Dorothy's nervous laughter over the awful truth.

* * *

Later in the week, Bishop Pascal prepared his sermon for the uncivilized outpost. The sin of pride would be the subject. He paced the spotless wooden floor of the resplendent library. Often his thoughts unfolded with movement. He would start with Job's sin of questioning the string of disasters God had deemed necessary for Job's edification. Who indeed could second guess the strong arm of God? Then he would caution the backwoods audience about their sins of pride, challenge them to look at the doubts they professed, or hid even from themselves. Like that precocious child who had been allowed unfettered use of this esteemed Jesuit collection of books.

She had no courses in the rigors of theological discussions. Her thinking could not stand the perils of belief long enough to sustain her faith. Great danger lay in following unguided thoughts, no matter what had triggered them. The devil could use the Bible as easily as he used his servants to become a stumbling block on the road to faith.

The horsehair couch beckoned the Bishop's aching knees. After easing himself down, the Bishop crossed his legs, taking notes of his inspirational thoughts on a clipboard made for the trip by a favorite Baltimore parishioner.

A nubile child such as Dorothy needed constant attention, strict supervision in order not to bring the faithful to perdition. Bishop Pascal lingered over the solution of turning her over his knee, spanking her into submission, lifting her skirts to administer the punishment more directly.

The Bishop stood, frightened by his impure thought. He smoothed down his wrinkled cassock, willing his body into submission. That was exactly what he wanted to prevent. Dorothy's lithe body called out to all the baser tendencies in men. She must be made aware of the mortal danger she was leading others to. To hell, surely. Dorothy needed to be rescued from God's favorite fallen angel. If she renewed her faith, surely the devil would stop using her to torture the saints. Like himself for pity's sake, the Bishop and head of the faithful.

* * *

When Father Sebastian answered the Bishop's message to come immediately to the library, he expected questions about dinner, or preparations for the trip around the Great Lakes. Instead he found the prelate agitated, face florid.

"Is there a cook I might take on the long trip?" The Bishop strode around the claw-footed library table, tapping its marble top with a long thumbnail.

"Elizabeth's quite settled here," Father Sebastian said. "I doubt she would abandon her daughter."

"Dorothy Evans?" The Bishop's voice bothered Sebastian.

"The girl we restricted from the library." Sebastian frowned at his feelings of dislike. Priests loved their Bishops. Surely it was required.

"Bright child, unfortunately," the Bishop mused.

"Very," Sebastian said, watchful.

"I might take her with us to Sister James Marine's school for young ladies." Bishop Pascal stopped encircling the table. "Would that be the best course of action?"

"I hardly know." Sebastian nose twitched. He stifled a sneeze. "I doubt her mother can spare her."

"Well," Bishop Pascal concluded the conversation as he left the room, "We can scarcely let a scholar remain a lowly kitchen maid."

"I guess not." Father Sebastian sadly reviewed the shelves of books Dorothy had enjoyed with such thoroughness.

* * *

Bishop Pascal had a harder time convincing Elizabeth to let her daughter finish her education at the Dominican convent.

"I can tell you right now she's not going to become a nun." Elizabeth slammed the oven shut.

"Dorothy seems hardly the type," Bishop Pascal admitted. "But surely you want a mind like hers put to better use?"

Elizabeth nodded. "I'm not that comfortable letting her go without me."

Bishop Pascal lifted his chin. "I'd be happy to vouch for her safety."

"Oh, it's not that," Elizabeth equivocated. "It's the trip and the dangers of hostile tribes."

"Father Sebastian assures me Ponthe Walker would easily stave off any trouble."

Elizabeth knew nothing could be done. Dorothy would want to go. Perish would be on the long trip. No harm would come to her and her daughter would jump at the chance to attend formal schooling. "Of course," Elizabeth said, dabbing at her eyes with her apron.

* * *

Dorothy was ecstatic, racing around their quarters, packing and unpacking five times, kissing and re-kissing her mother. "I can really go? You'll explain to Beauty. Perhaps I can spend next winter with her."

Now she could prove to everyone, especially herself, that she could live as an innocent, one with nature. Was the Lord blessing her? She no longer needed to feel guilty about being white, stealing land and the very air from the natives. In nature she could serve others. Cooking would be a matter of survival. Dorothy felt needed, giving her energy to others. She'd be serving Perish his meals -- almost like being his wife.

Her good mood seeped into her dreams at night. She dreamt of a cathedral of trees. Stained glass windows let the color-dimmed light sweep a floor of trillium vines. Their white trumpet flowers, tinged in hues from the windows, offered up a heady scent. Choral music from female voices drifted through the branches of the trees where answering birds and blue butterflies rose to a ceiling of revolving stars. Candles and chandeliers hid the walls with their flickering soft flames of prayer. The cushioned benches were filled with rows and rows of books. The aisles were lined with sleeping forest animals. Quail and deer lay side by side with rabbits and raccoons. Mice and possum blinked in silence next to porcupines and otter. A black bear lazily swatted at a butterfly on its nose.

On the altar, dinner was set with golden plates and silver chalices. Towering rainbow banks of flowers with trailing crescendos of wild roses and violets were arranged down the center of the incredibly long table. Bearded apostles stood at their places. The center seat was empty, but Dorothy didn't need to inquire. The Son of God, Jesus of Nazareth, would return. Dorothy was content to wait, hoping He'd appear shortly.

Her eyes were drawn to innumerable books sitting primly in their pews, row after row of them. Dorothy's fingers yearned to open each one. Above the smell of freshness and flowers she thought she could smell the glue of book bindings, their rich leather covers, the pages themselves...all new, all promising. When she sighed with pleasure at her imagined heaven, she woke.

* * *

All through her morning chores Dorothy floated in her dream world. She tried not to speak to her mother's kitchen helpers lest she lose one detail of the dream.

Blue Feather and High Call, the daughters of Chechalk and Crane, recognized her trance, touching her shoulder before directing her attention without words to the burning bacon and the thickening oatmeal.

Elizabeth scowled at her scatter-brained daughter. "Head in the cloud will destroy the Bishop's last meal."

Dorothy smiled to accept the admonishment.

"She's dreaming of her new husband." Papikitcha, Flat Belly's wife, giggled to the younger girls.

Blue Feather started to laugh with High Call, who nearly spilled a pitcher of cooled milk.

"Outside, Dorothy," Elizabeth commanded. "Go see if the canoes have sprung leaks."

Dorothy bolted out the kitchen's back door. She didn't need much more of an invitation to seek out Perish. Compare visions. Her mouth watered strangely. Did he dream of her?

Fort Detroit's military inhabitants hadn't yet been roused by the trumpet's morning call. The central parade ground was empty of their lounging clutter. A few dogs stretched to identify her scent. One ambled beside her to the compound's side-door. The massive front gates were shut at sunset as part of the flag-lowering ceremony. None of the high-tension stories of the past war years seemed possible in the peacefully dawning day.

Dorothy patted the soft fur of the trotting sheepdog next to her. He licked her hand with his wet, rough tongue as she stepped outside. The smell of vegetation freshened Dorothy's lungs from the smoky kitchen shed. Daybreak fed the dark blue clouds with peach-tinged highlights. The lake stayed a silvery dark mass, unrelieved by tones of blue from the sky. The birds reminded her of her perfect dream heaven.

Her body quickened to life when she pondered where Perish slept the night before. Did a blanket on the grass suffice? Was she too young for him to consider as a mate? Her heart sped up its beat and her stomach asked for breakfast, or his comfort. She wanted to run as fast as her eager legs could carry her the half-mile to the riverbank, to him.

Under a leaf-stripped willow, Dorothy spotted his silhouette. His clothes and stance labeled him native. The absence of daylight hid his paleface hair. The stories of bold and dangerous natives played with her nerves. The mere sight of him seemed to pull her in his direction as if a he had thrown a rope out to fetch her.

He turned when he heard her approach. Then irritated by some internal prompting, he punched the canoe laying face down next to him.

"Mother asked me to see if the canoes had any holes in them." She laughed at her delight in finding him. "And here you are damaging our vessels."

He didn't flinch at her remark.

He's transfixed by me, she thought. "I can help you turn it over." She spoke more quietly to him.

Perish frowned. "It's fine the way it is."

"Did you hear I'm the cook for the journey?" Dorothy stood opposite him with the canoe between them.

"Bishop Pascal wants you educated in a religious school."

Dorothy reached across the boat to touch his arm. Of course, he misunderstood. Her reach didn't span the canoe. "Not to become a nun, just for the education."

Perish moved to her side of the boat. He met her eyes and took her hand.

She moved closer to him, sweeping one of his blond braids behind his shoulder. His arm went around her waist pulling her to his solid chest. She moved her hand around his neck, and he bent his mouth to hers. The warmth of her body distilled into her lips at the soft touch of his lips. He seemed glued to their tender kiss. Every worry about his roughness vanished. Here was a gentle man, needing her.

At a noise in the direction of the fort, Perish put distance between them.

Dorothy reluctantly let go.

"The trip up-country will be difficult in the winter," Perish said. His eyes still held her.

"I'm strong," Dorothy said. "When the others get lazy, I chop wood for Mother."

Ponthe joined the young couple. "Trying to discourage the new recruit?"

Perish blushed.

"He's afraid I'm weak." Dorothy wondered as Perish surely did, if Ponthe had seen them kiss.

Ponthe said, "There are dangers strength can't surmount."

"I can learn what I need to know." Dorothy wasn't buying any of that old males can, females can't nonsense.

"Do you swim well under the ice?" Ponthe asked deadpan.

"No," Dorothy's voice faltered, then she recognized the joke. "Because I'll never have to."

Ponthe winked at her, as if she was a child.

"You hope." Perish smiled a dimpled grin. "I'm glad you're coming. Everyone else is so old."

Ponthe had his turn to frown. "Your friends are old? Jimmy Sweetwater is a moon younger, Lieutenant Cass maybe two years older, and Henry Holt is younger than Dorothy."

"Jimmy's not weaned from alcohol, Henry still plays with tops. I suppose Lieutenant Cass realizes which side is up for a canoe. How old are you?" Perish asked Dorothy.

"I may not be old, but I'm competent." Dorothy's chin tilted up.

"And prideful." Bishop Pascal had strolled up to them on the soft grass.

The hand he placed on Dorothy's shoulder made her shudder from his cold fingertips. Dorothy noticed Ponthe smiled to himself, but Perish did not.

"It will be hard work," Perish said.

"Dorothy's accustomed to that," the Bishop said.

Dorothy moved away from the Bishop's touch by stepping to the side and pushing her hair behind her ears.

The Bishop turned to watch her, then asked Ponthe, "When do you think we will reach Fort Meigs? I need to make arrangements for a stage coach to take me to Philadelphia after the trip."

Ponthe shook his head. "If the trails are dry, we could be there by the third month of summer."

"No sooner than August?" Bishop Pascal asked. "That's nearly a year."

Dorothy could not help her surprise. "That long!" She tried to catch a look at Perish, but his braids hid his expression.

"Your shoes won't make the trip," Perish said.

Dorothy looked down at her slippers. "I can buy boots like yours."

"Beauty made mine," Perish said eye-to-eye with her.

Dorothy could feel the warmth of his look. Did he recognize that she hated the Bishop's touch? She smiled at him, hoping he understood.

"We won't have time for that." Ponthe had interpreted their silent communication.

"I have money saved," Dorothy said, reluctantly turning away from her strong attraction to Perish's dimple. She hoped the limited supplies at the trade post would offer up a pair of boots.

"Fort Meigs will have enough supplies to reclothe you for Philadelphia," Bishop Pascal said.

"Mother has that all figured out," Dorothy smiled back at Perish, not the Bishop. "She's shipping a trunk of my things to be held at the fort."

"Good thinking," Ponthe said.

* * *

Perish couldn't believe the number of weeks involved in organizing the group's trip. He was more than ready to be with Dorothy every day for nearly a year. Tension settled on his shoulders, making his feet restless to be on their way. However, Ponthe took his time deciding whether each article of clothing, each pot of Dorothy's, each book of the Bishop's, each carton of ammunition for hunting game should be carried in the canoes. Two days were wasted in repacking and arguing about particulars. Perish wanted to kick them all the way to Lake Erie before anyone was ready.

"One change of clothing and one winter coat." Ponthe threw Jimmy Sweetwater's extra coat onto a nearby rock.

They all heard the bottles break.

"You sure you can make this trip dry," Perish asked.

Jimmy weaved toward his discarded, dripping coat. "Guess I'll find out."

Ponthe took two of the small pots out of Dorothy's soup kettle. "Too heavy. A coffee pot, fry pan and one soup kettle. Tie the handles together when you put them in the canoe."

Dorothy remained her cheerful self. "I thought you were concerned with space, not weight."

After looking through her waterproof satchel of clothing Ponthe seemed to approve. "Good job."

Then Perish shared Dorothy's dismay as Ponthe pulled out a string of bagged herbs.

"And this?"

"Is needed so the soup doesn't taste like the kettle."

Perish admired her witty defense. Here was a girl who could keep a quiet evening before a campfire interesting. His body let down a few defenses and Perish was not surprised at its feral response to his thoughts.

Bishop Pascal didn't look particularly serene when Ponthe unpacked the stack of books the prelate had lined his bag with.

"Your memory," Ponthe said, "and the Bible will have to do."

"I can't survive without the written word."

"I won't send men swimming for these books when the canoe turns over." Ponthe patted Perish's shoulder.

Dorothy moved closer to Perish. "Will the boat turn over?"

"Usually," Ponthe said, examining Lieutenant Cass backpack.

"I really can't swim," Dorothy whispered to Perish.

He couldn't let her drown, not after she'd passed his father's packing rules. "I'll watch out for you."

She smiled up at him.

Her confidence in him swelled his chest. She trusted him. He wished they were together in some secret cove away from this yammering crowd. He would take her hand.... Perish hooked his thumb into the last row of quills on his vest.

"Okay," Ponthe directed. "Everyone empty your pockets."

Bishop Pascal laid his reading glasses and a watch on the overturned canoe.

"You'll need a string around those glasses to keep them attached to your neck. The watch can be shipped to Fort Meigs."

Perish presented his new medicine bag. The red-spotted beaded bag held herbs and tea leaves. Beauty had given it to him before she returned to her Raisin River home.

Ponthe nodded, probably recognizing the handiwork.

Lieutenant Cass had a small telescope. "I know only God sees tomorrow, but I like to see a few yards ahead of me in new country."

"Wrap something around the thing and tie it to your knife belt," Ponthe instructed.

Ponthe patted all of Jimmy Sweetwater's pockets. He found a bag of chewing tobacco. "Good enough," he said to a grateful smile from Jimmy.

Henry Holt's pockets held marvelous things: a feather from a goldfinch, candle ends, a tin of matches, a knife, four buttons, a top, a pair of dice, and a living toad.

Ponthe shook his head. "Good luck coming home with that stuff," was all he said.

Perish was sure Henry would blush with embarrassment. His collection showed that he was still a boy.

However, Henry was unfazed. "I'm the only one that passed," he said.

Perish wished Ponthe had commented on Dorothy's inappropriate dress. How could he keep her safe with all those petticoats tangling into everything? And the perfume would bring mosquitoes from the next three rivers. His body could attest to her fragrance's attraction potential.

* * *

The morning of their departure Bishop Pascal was the first to object to Dorothy's attire. "That will never do, young lady."

Dorothy didn't care if he liked it or not. "Mother says I look like a well-seasoned camper."

Ponthe approached smiling and nodding. "I know that beadwork. Beauty has given you a gift of many hours."

"Yes." Dorothy breath stopped when Perish took his first step in her direction. The most important male on the trip approved. She couldn't ask for more. "At least I can move without getting my skirts in the campfire."

* * *

Perish moved in even closer. A new schism entered his world. Joy danced through his veins. Beauty had replicated the dress of the woman floating in his Copper Harbor vision for Dorothy. He needed no other message of Beauty's approval of his courtship. He touched the red circles of beadwork worked into the shoulders of Dorothy's form-fitting, white deerskin dress. Instead of petticoats, a short fringe flirted with the tops of Dorothy's new boots.

He flared his nostrils and moved downwind of her. No scent of any kind. "You look more native than I do."

"Exactly," Bishop Pascal huffed. "You come along with me, child. Your mother has some answering to do."

"Bishop," Ponthe took the Bishop's ringed hand off of Dorothy's forearm. "We're putting the boats in the water right now."

Bishop Pascal marched away without Dorothy. "We'll see about this."

"Bishop," Ponthe patiently called. "If you want a say in these treaty negotiations, I would reconsider the importance of missing petticoats."

The Bishop stopped. "Her safety is in your hands."

Dorothy smiled at Perish, whispering, "It always had been."

Chapter Three

Trip to Point Pelee

Once they were launched on the Detroit River, the largest canoe led the way. The Bishop pulled his paddle on the same side as Henry and Crane. Jimmy Sweetwater, Flat Belly, and Lieutenant Cass manned the opposite side. Perish and Dorothy were in the second smaller canoe. Ponthe deftly kept his large supply loaded canoe in their lee.

Dorothy tried to mimic Perish's strokes, but she couldn't pull her own weight through the water. About all she could manage was to balance against the waves with the paddle. She handled her terror of falling into the water by watching Perish's yellow braids sweep across his broad shoulders. She imagined them sweeping across her face in some future lodge, after they married. How could she even think of their future? Why would he pick her for a wife? For a lifetime together, what would she bring of value? Penniless, without any hope of inheritance, her heart, intellect, and the promise of many healthy children were her only assets.

The extensive portage around the rapids into Lake Erie, left Dorothy hoping the trip had already ended. Her arms ached from her ineffective paddling in the river, and once on dry land her new boots protested against the rock filled paths. The first few days must be the hardest, she reasoned. She refused to give a voice to any of her aches and pains, unlike the Bishop.

"Stop," he demanded before drinking from his water pouch. "Surely we need to eat." He was next to last in the line of hikers. "It must be two o'clock by now."

"Not noon." Crane pushed the prelate's shoulders forward.

Ponthe took pity on the prelate, calling from under his shouldered canoe, "We'll have food once we reach Point Pelee. If you paddle hard enough, we might be there by two."

Lake Erie's blue-green expanse awed Dorothy. No land was visible toward the northeast. Time was taken to drop trolling nets in the water from each of the three canoes to catch Blue Pike and

Walleye fish. The prevailing west winds helped the current push the canoes to their wooded destination.

Dorothy had wanted to share her cathedral dream with Perish before it dimmed completely. But there didn't seem to be enough time between cooking, sleeping, and packing. Besides, in the canoe, Perish's back couldn't show his reaction to the glory of her dream's tree-lined church, the blue butterflies. She wanted to see his dimple, as she mentioned the passive beasts of the forest.

* * *

The sun warmed Perish's back, or the thought of Dorothy an arm-span behind him, provided the heat. At one point, she nodded off and dropped her paddle. Ponthe rescued it, paddling forward to hand it to Perish.

Ponthe made hand signals, stirring a pot to signify Dorothy. Then he moved an invisible spoon to his mouth and rubbed his stomach. Perish understood he was to let the cook sleep so she would have enough energy to prepare a tasty meal.

Perish agreed, stashing the precious paddle under the seat. He hoped Dorothy would cook another stew. His stomach was beginning to show signs of his head being cut off. It growled in dismay.

After they reached Point Pelee, Dorothy asked Ponthe, "Should I fix more?" The pan-fried biscuits and bacon disappeared quickly among the three interpreters, three natives, Perish, and the Bishop.

"No," Ponthe said. "Too much food for hikers makes us act like dogs. We eat ourselves into a stupor."

"I'll take Crane with me to find a campsite and meat for tonight," Perish offered.

Ponthe nodded, repositioning his canoe carriers. "Bishop, give Dorothy your pack. Take Lieutenant Cass' place under the big canoe."

Lieutenant Cass hefted Perish's canoe. "Light work," he laughed, letting it gently back down to the grass.

Perish reached up to clap his shoulder. "Keep my baby safe."

"Which one?" Lieutenant Cass teased.

* * *

Dorothy was pleased to see Perish's color rise. He wasn't dangerous, just defensive about his lack of experience with women. Her thoughts became entangled in a future scene where they would have equal pleasure in discovering each other. She dropped the coffee pot, spilling the contents out into the fire.

"Easier ways to put out a fire." Flat Belly scooped dirt on the rest of the flames with his moccasin. "Save the cold coffee for me next time."

Within several minutes Crane and Perish returned to the noon-day camp.

"We have company," Perish said to his father.

Behind him, eight Seneca leaders entered their campsite.

Ponthe stepped forward. "Captain Signore and Big Turtle, introduce me to your delegates."

The oldest member of the group, who wore a battered French officer's coat, turned to his group. "My youngest brother, Dasquorant; my brother chief, Civil John; and my sister, Clan Mother, Sacoureweeghta, or Whipping Stick."

The giant introduced as Signore's youngest brother evaluated their group. His eyes slipped over the three white interpreters, dismissing them as unimportant. Crane and Flat Belly were granted a modicum of interest. The Bishop's presence was noted briefly, and then Dasquorant stood unmoving, his gaze level with a spot, slightly higher than Ponthe's head. Dorothy thought he purposely ignored Perish and herself. She was wrong.

The short and broad older woman, Clan Mother, walked directly to Dorothy. She whispered, "Call me Whipping Stick."

Dorothy whispered her name in return, "Dorothy Evans, cook."

Ponthe and Signore stopped the introductions, turning toward the two women.

Dorothy touched Perish's shoulder. "Did I make a mistake?"

Whipping Stick laughed. "Not you, little sister."

The native named Civil John tapped his walking staff on the sand. "Ponthe, you know our ways. Clan Mother will name us for you."

Ponthe touched his forehead in apology.

Whipping Stick motioned for the three remaining members of her group to step forward. "Aquasheno, you may call 'Joe'; and this is Skilleway or 'Robin'."

Robin resembled his namesake bird down to his red vest, bobbing head and straggly coat tails.

Whipping Stick purposefully pulled Perish out from behind Ponthe as a sign that he was equal to his father. Then she introduced a blue-eyed man, "and Wakenuceno, my adopted son, William Spicer. You may call him 'White Man'."

The eight new arrivals arranged themselves around the dead campfire.

Perish motioned for Dorothy to follow him into the woods behind the campsite on the triangle of sand known as Point Pelee.

Dasquorant, the giant, noticed and called after them, "Don't wander off to amuse yourselves."

Ponthe intervened. "He's discussing lunch with the cook."

Perish took Dorothy's hand as he explained the situation. "We have to feed them while they sit down to talk about the treaty. We can't let them leave without feeding them."

'I have to crouch in front of all of them to remake the fire and cook?" Dorothy had never felt shy before. "The giant...."

Perish turned from gathering kindling. "Who? I'll help."

"Nothing, nothing." Dorothy gathered her pride and courage closer to her. Beauty's deerskin dress comforted her. The group recognized by the intricate beadwork on the dress that she was already honored by a native artisan.

Trying to create a world veiled off from the circle of strangers, Dorothy went to work, restarting the fire. After frying more bacon, she made cornmeal pan biscuits. She cut up the fried bacon and made a tomato and bean stew, seasoned with her herbs to prepare the visitors a better lunch than she and the rest of the crew had just eaten.

Crane, with his long neck bowed, and Flat Belly, bending at the waist, served each of the Seneca tribe members a bowl of food while Captain Signore and Ponthe discussed the treaty, with occasional questions from Bishop Pascal.

Captain Signore bowed his head to Whipping Stick before beginning. "We have 83 to provide for."

"How many will meet at the rapids?" Bishop Pascal asked.

The Clan Mother held up her hand. "Black Skirt, in my tribe the women consult their men in private."

Ponthe explained, "Bishop Pascal is of the same family of French Jesuit missionaries who sent Father Louis Nicolas."

Whipping Stick considered a string of wampum she carried. "Too long ago for me to know."

"Yes, Clan Mother," Ponthe used her respectful title. "Too long. He was a man who hid behind the long skirt, too."

"Why do they?" Whipping Stick asked, unmindful of the Bishop's discomfort.

Bishop Pascal tried to explain. "We don't use women. We keep our bodies pure for the Great Spirit's use."

Whipping Stick seemed to ponder on the fact. "For how many months?"

"Forever," the Bishop answered, counting his redemption finished.

"Too long," the old woman said. "Make you sick in the head finally. Your wishes will come out crooked, maybe evil."

Dorothy caught Perish looking at her. They agreed. Ponthe coughed.

Captain Signore guided the discussion back to the treaty. "The eight you see before you will attend the conference."

"Our reservation land in New York State is not large enough to feed us," Civil John said sadly. "Some of our young people have asked Dasquorant to take them to the Great Plains."

The old woman shrank with grief and shame.

When Dorothy handed the corn cakes around, Dasquorant leveled an angry look at her. With a sympathetic glance, Dorothy tried to say she understood his anger at white people for stealing the land. The giant turned away disgusted with her.

Ponthe explained the terms of the proposed treaty. "Perish, hang the map between those two saplings."

The cheerful looking Seneca, Robin, helped with the chore.

With deference shown to Whipping Stick, Ponthe marked the future Seneca site. "As I showed Big Turtle and Captain Signore while they were with me in Washington, the Lower Sandusky River shore is your future home. A section of 640 acres will be set aside for the tribe, and another section of 640 acres for the trade post of William Spicer. Also an additional 30,000 acres to Spicer. He married a member of your tribe."

"Spicer?" Joe asked. "Clan Mother, is that your white son's name?"

"Yes," she said, quietly head bowed

"The Great White Father's representatives convinced us he would be taken care of by the tribal allocation," Big Turtle said.

Dasquorant stood. "Who is the Seneca woman Spicer married?"

Whipping Stick stood to give her answer. Her age and bulk required a little time to accomplish the feat. "Me," she said. "William Spicer, or White Man, is marrying me."

White Man, about the same age as Perish, had also finished his meal. He walked to where Dasquorant faced the tablecloth map. "We needed more land, brother."

Dasquorant recoiled with the remark. "Brother," he growled, as if the word was made of broken glass.

"Will we have enough time to re-bury the dead at this new site?" White Man asked. "Before we move our village?"

"Plenty of time after the treaty conference," Bishop Pascal said.

Civil John shook his head. "If the treaty holds that long."

"The Great White Father needs the peace," Bishop Pascal pontificated.

Ponthe raised his hand, then pointed palm up to Perish. "Earlier this year when we visited the government rooms in Washington, my son uncovered the reason Monroe needs a new treaty."

No one moved.

A fly buzzed around the giant's head, but he didn't flick an eyelash. Attention was focused on Perish's father.

But Perish spoke. "A canal big enough to float wagons will be built into the land from the Hudson River to Lake Erie. Farmers coming here in those wagons want the land and the peace needed to tend their crops."

Ponthe looked at the ground, then straightened his shoulders. Shielding his eyes, he noted the hour by the sun. "I hope to reach all the tribes left in the Old Northwest by the end of next summer. The Great White Father Monroe is sending his commissioners and agents to the foot of the rapids of the Maumee River that feeds Lake Erie. Clan Mother, the Seneca tribe, as keeper of the eastern door of the Iroquois, is the first to see the plans."

"How many tribes are left?" White Man asked.

Ponthe answered, "We will meet the Huron after we cross the Thames River, the Ottawa at Fort Mackinac, the Delaware at Sturgeon Bay, the Potawatomi at Fort Dearborn in Illinois Territory, then the Shawnee in St. Louis, and the Chippewa at Fort Wayne."

* * *

Perish bowed his head in respect for the native nations gone from the earth: the Mohawk, the Illinois, the Fox, and the Maumee. Only the rivers kept the names of proud people dispersed to the west or farther than feet could carry, into the clouds. Some part of him, the greedy part, had stepped on humans too troublesome to include in Mother Earth's bounty. He must be careful not to let the evil in his blood corrupt his life or anyone he came in contact with. Did Dorothy feel this same remorse?

Her silent stance next to the pile of food supplies led him to believe she knew the despair the once proud people must have experienced. Now they were divided and scattered to the winds. Dorothy raised her head and gasped when she realized he had been studying her.

Not with hate, he wanted to shout. He grinned, hoping his affection, for the slim girl, dressed modestly in Indian attire, would cross the campsite. Her black braids and tanning skin made her appear more native than he. His lifetime spent living among the natives had taught him 'adopted' didn't mean belonging. Even the white man's allowance of 30,640 acres didn't appease all the Seneca members. The sin was too great to cover with gifts.

"So they bribe us with a beaver pond when we own the lake." Whipping Stick said, resigned to the inevitable.

"Thank you, Clan Mother, for bringing your delegates to us." Ponthe sat down with the sad older woman. "You have saved us a week of travel."

"I've been called impatient all my life," Whipping Stick grinned and motioned for Dorothy to join them. "When I was your age, maybe younger, nothing could keep me from doing what I pleased."

"I have that problem," Dorothy ducked her head.

Whipping Stick put her palm under Dorothy's chin. "Keep it. Why make a liar out of people?" She laughed. "I used to throw things at the old chief, my husband. He died with Tecumseh." She laughed again. "At least I never had children." Then she whispered to Dorothy. "He was afraid of me. Don't be like that."

"Is White Man really your husband?" Perish asked.

"Hmm. He loves me like a mother." Whipping Stick looked longing at her young, virile husband as he untied the bedding rolls. "I'm too old for children anyway."

"I want children," Dorothy said. "I'm an only child."

"How many?" Whipping Stick asked. "I know a woman with 20."

"Twenty! Six would be nice." Dorothy said.

Perish was eavesdropping on woman talk. He turned his back and walked away, still chewing on the fact that Dorothy wanted six children. How could he keep six children fed with the Old Northwest's game diminishing by the day? Only white men earned enough money in 1817 to feed that many children. Maybe he could become a government-paid Indian agent and man a trading post at Raisin River. Would Ponthe approve?

* * *

Whipping Stick stroked her own plump chin. "After you have six children, at the new year, when the light has to fight the darkness, offer a small white dog to the gods, then name the sixth child after me, if it's a girl."

Dorothy hoped her eyes didn't betray her distress at the name, Whipping Stick. "Of course," she said.

Whipping Stick smiled wickedly. "After I'm dead I'll haunt you if you lie." She laughed as Dorothy's eyes got even bigger. "Call her Susan, and I'll know that is your way of naming her Sacoureweeghta."

Dorothy was thoroughly shamed. "I'll put your name on her baptismal document, and call her Susan. How do you spell your real name?"

Whipping Stick motioned for White Man to join them. "Spell my name for Dorothy, so she can name a child after me."

White Man pulled a bound pad from his pocket. The paper was held between birch bark covers. He wrote 'Sacoureweeghta' in plain bold letters. "If you name a town after your daughter, make sure they know it is the name of a proud line of Seneca."

Dorothy realized the man loved his native mother, now his wife. After he walked away, she whispered as low as she could to Whipping Stick. "I hope someone will love me as much as White Man loves you."

Whipping Stick made a girlish gesture of denial. "Men never leave women, remember that. Don't change who you are by their promptings. They'll get you to be just who they think they want, then find out they liked you better in the beginning."

"My mother and father were both white." Dorothy wanted to make that clear to her, although she wasn't sure why it seemed important.

"And you think only Perish North's father was native?"

"How do you know all that?"

"I don't. I see who interests you." Whipping Stick nudged her arm.

Bishop Pascal had been listening. "Perish was raised as an Indian. You, however, young lady, have been raised in a civilized environment."

"Up to now," Whipping Stick said. "Now she knows how to give her heart."

The Bishop started to move away, but Whipping Stick called to him, "Bishop, I have a story for you."

"A parable," Ponthe interpreted to focus the Bishop's attention.

White Man brought a blanket to wrap around Whipping Stick's shoulders as she spoke. The wind swell from Lake Erie had cooled off the beach. Perish and Robin fed the fire with more wood. Sparks lifted to the darkening sky. Crane passed a lit pipe to Flat Belly.

Whipping Stick began, "Many years ago a young girl got very sick in our long house. Our medicine man wore his bent-nose mask for two days near her bed. His tortoiseshell rattles did no good. The young girl wouldn't eat. The medicine man drew his own blood, offered beads and tobacco to the parents, but nothing worked. Her parents asked her what would make her happy, now that she was near death. The sick girl asked for the pet cat of the Chief's daughter. It was happily given by the Chief who didn't want any of his tribe to suffer from thwarted wishes. The sick girl recovered, but the daughter of the Chief died."

"What does it mean?" the Bishop asked Ponthe.

"Ask me," Whipping Stick said. "It means if you don't use your sex it will drop off."

The Bishop blanched.

Ponthe rose and tried to change the subject. "The sun is racing to set. We need to make camp among the trees for shelter. We can get an early start to meet with the Hurons at the Thames River crossing."

"I will serve mass at daybreak," Bishop Pascal said. "Dorothy, Henry, Lieutenant Cass, I can hear your confessions now."

Henry wrinkled his nose and ran for the woods. Lieutenant Cass and Dorothy exchanged glances. Neither of them trusted the man; nevertheless, the teachings from when they were children kicked in.

Lieutenant Cass leaned over to say quietly for only Dorothy's ear. "Even though I am sure God is reconciled to us, I'll appease the old man." He followed the Bishop closer to the end of Point Pelee.

Perish came up behind Dorothy. "Do you have to tell him we kissed?"

"No, but I have had impure thoughts about you." Dorothy worried about telling the truth to the Bishop. "I wish Father Sebastian was here."

Perish was all smiles. "Impure thoughts. Like what?"

"None of your business." Dorothy grinned at her ornery man.

Whipping Stick looked directly at them, enjoying the young couple's shenanigans. "Ponthe," she called.

Ponthe dutifully came to her side.

"Go tell that cross old man: Dorothy's confessor is back at Fort Detroit."

"I won't be able to take communion," Dorothy said.

"Just as well," Ponthe said. "You can hear mass with the rest of us sinners."

A slight touch on Dorothy's cheekbone was familiar. Her guardian angel always rewarded her with a kiss when her actions pleased. "I'd be glad to be part of the group," Dorothy said. A warm glow filled her from the affection of those around her. Only one person disapproved of her, and she disapproved of him. Not his profession, just the man himself seemed wrong in the administration of his duties, off kilter, twisted like a snake in the fork of sensuous tree limbs.

Whipping Stick called to the Seneca men, "Let's smoke to our agreement."

When Lieutenant Cass returned, Ponthe set out to dismiss the confessional session. The Bishop came back to camp as the sacred pipe was being passed to Dorothy. He gave her a look that was supposed to condemn her soul, but the joy of communion with the campfire guests erased his censure. The tobacco made her cough.

About a mile inland from the point, the Seneca started a fire pit for their evening camp. Close by, Perish and Crane ringed their fire with lake stones. Dorothy left the Seneca with their feet to the fire pit. Perish had positioned her bedroll between Ponthe and himself. Confident of her safety, Dorothy sought out a private place to prepare for the evening.

As she straightened her pantaloons under the buckskin dress, Bishop Pascal called softly from a bank of bushes behind her. "Dorothy Evans, when you're finished, I need a word."

No avoiding the lecture, Dorothy told herself.

His face appeared darkly shadowed in the evening's twilight. He stroked the crucifix on his chest with series of long caresses, increasing with his agitation.

Dorothy steeled herself for his onslaught of words.

"You are being corrupted by these people. You have already degenerated into a savage, wanton hussy. Dasquorant can't take his evil eyes off you. You know Perish and his father are quite besotted with you." The Bishop seemed to have trouble breathing.

She wished he'd at least stop stroking the cross.

"You bend over the fire with your curves clearly visible through your dress. Even your sleeves reveal too much of your," the Bishop's voice dropped an octave, "shapely arms."

Dorothy backed away in the direction of the campsite, she hoped.

"You will go to hell if you keep bedeviling God with your temptress ways. Walk without swaying your hips, fold your arms when you walk. You bring the godly to their knees." The Bishop dropped at the word.

Dasquorant had a firm grip on the shoulder of the Bishop forcing him to remain kneeling. "Join the others," the giant said quietly to her. "Send Ponthe."

Dorothy turned and seeing the light from Ponthe's campfire, ran toward safety unmindful of the bushes and branches tearing at her hair, scratching her face. "Ponthe," she choked. "Ponthe, Dasquorant needs you. The Bishop...."

Ponthe jumped to his feet. He disappeared in the direction Dorothy had come.

Perish rushed to her side.

Dorothy could see the other campsite roused by her disturbance.

"Please," she said to Perish. "I must sit down." Her legs crumbled beneath her. "I'm so tired."

* * *

Perish helped her to her bedroll, took off her boots and commanded she rest her head for the night.

When she fell immediately to sleep, Whipping Stick invited the other Seneca to return to their fire.

"Ponthe will handle this," she said. "From now on, Perish, the Bishop must not voice his evil to Dorothy Evans."

"Yes, Clan Mother." Perish hoped Ponthe throttled the man.

Perish waited and when Ponthe returned, Perish told him, "Clan Mother says the Bishop must never speak to Dorothy again."

"Exactly." Ponthe reclined on the other side of Dorothy. "Dasquorant and I just convinced the man only his silence was required on the trip."

"Perhaps Dasquorant should escort him back to Fort Detroit."

"We need his approval of the negotiations for Washington." Ponthe turned away to sleep.

Perish knew he should rest; instead he kept guard, watching the innocent girl at his side.

Evil did exist, but it didn't need his lack of vigilance to feed it. Dorothy's face was briefly lit by the campfire. How could anyone, especially a man dedicated to good, assume that face meant harm to anyone? The flames played with her familiar features and he drifted into sleep.

* * *

In the morning, Dorothy tried to serve left-over corncakes to the Seneca.

"Food of the dead," Dasquorant said, tossing it to the ground.

Captain Signore came to Dorothy's rescue. "Not everyone knows our ways, younger brother."

Whipping Stick joined in. "We believe food made the day before belongs to the dead. It is poison to the living."

Dorothy apologized, "I'll make fresh."

"No need," Whipping Stick said. "We must leave. For one last time I need to see the Genesee River gorge, where we hill-people were born. Then we will rest at Red House Lake before taking the Allegheny River route back to our reservation. I will offer tobacco to the sky spirit to keep your treaty-trip safe."

"I wish I had something to give to you," Dorothy said.

"See, Dasquorant, her heart does know our ways." Whipping Stick hugged her. "I will give you a gift, Ponthe. Take this strong young man with you. His feet need the trail."

Ponthe seemed to understand. "Dasquorant, do you wish to come with us?"

Without hesitation Dasquorant answered. "Clan Mother holds our wishes close to her heart. I'm strong and may be of service."

Because Dasquourunt's elder made the request, Perish was not surprised at the surly giant's willingness to bear their burdens. Perish did worry Dasquourunt might appear a better woodsman than he. Why was he concerned? Of course, Dorothy's opinion mattered. He accepted the element of competition in courtship. The Lord would help, he hoped. Otherwise, why had he seen Dorothy and heard her promise of generations to come in his manhood vision?

The tribe assembled to say their good-byes.

Whipping Stick stood with her outstretched arms on the shoulders of Perish and Dorothy. "See you when it's time to make the Green Corn Ceremony, or at least before the Harvest Festival."

Perish knew the blessing. It was almost a contract for Dorothy, Whipping Stick, and himself. He would need to lay down his life for Dorothy in order to bring her safely to Whipping Stick at the treaty powwow.

"Good-bye," Whipping Stick said to the silent Bishop. "Mind your ways, Atotarho, before it's time for you to be judged."

To Perish's ears, and the rest of the natives, the words were not merely an indictment. The words meant Bishop Pascal's life was in mortal danger. He wouldn't see the Green Corn Ceremony. All Clan Mothers possessed this inner gift of sight.

Chapter Four

Thames River Crossing

President Monroe's treaty-hawkers left Point Pelee's forest, heading inland toward the northern crossing of the Thames River. Dorothy breathed in the sweet fresh smell. Browning alfalfa fields and wild grasses stretched in every direction on the Ontario Peninsula between Lake Erie and Lake Huron. The load of supplies on Dorothy's back got heavier with each mile. When her thirst wasn't quenched by sips from Perish's water bag, she picked a dried stalk of pepper weed to bring saliva to her mouth. The sun wasn't hot but a steady wind made her squint. Katydids and an occasional gull provided music for the quiet trail. Dorothy could see rain falling on the western horizon in dark blue slants.

Perish walked beside her with his arms above his head to balance the small canoe. At one point he stopped, laying the canoe on its side. His muscles rippled as he stretched out a cramp in his arm. He came close to check her pack. As he added a head strap, Dorothy smelled his heated body with its hint of juniper. Joy leapt unbidden, spreading contentment where toil had left its mark. They were together, surely forever.

A crisply defined rainbow appeared opposite the rain clouds. As Dorothy started to point, Perish saw the splendor, too. He swung her uplifted arm to his shoulder and wound his free arm around her waist.

The affection Dorothy detected in the warmth of his kiss lightened her burden even more. "You like me," she said.

"Yep," he said and reloaded his canoe to his shoulders.

As they rounded a bend in the path, the line of campers stretched out. Dorothy counted them. First in line, loose-limbed Henry Holt beat the dry grass with a stick to warn snakes or hiding birds because people were invading their peaceful domain. Bishop Pascal with his head bowed shambled behind Henry. Then the big canoe followed, hoisted over the heads of Dasquorant, Lieutenant Cass, Crane and Flat Belly. Each man involved in the portage carried a pack of supplies on his back. Dorothy was glad she didn't have to shoulder a canoe. Jimmy Sweetwater followed Perish and Dorothy. Jimmy helped carry Ponthe's supply canoe.

Dorothy tried to curb her elation at Perish's ministrations. She wasn't as significant in his life as she wanted to be...someday. After all, his friendliness extended to each member on the trek with the exception of Bishop Pascal and maybe the giant, Dasquorant. But he hadn't kissed them.

"Who's more white?" she asked him. "You or me?"

"Only my mother was white," Perish said. "My father was Potawatomi with the name of North. Ponthe is Huron. You look more Indian than I do."

"My mother left a Methodist minister." Dorothy laughed. "I doubt he was a native."

"And your mother's family?"

She loved his grin. Nothing was as sweet as that ornery dimple on his right cheek. "All white, I'm afraid."

Perish surveyed his moving feet for a few steps. "Why did your mother desert your father?"

"Evil." Dorothy pointed in Bishop Pascal's direction. "Religions sometimes make people identify other creatures as less worthy than themselves. Not Father Sebastian."

Ponthe came up behind them and said while passing, "Don't lag behind, you two."

Perish bent over with his hands on his knees to catch his breath. "Did he beat her?"

"He berated her," Dorothy said. "I'm sure she had enough presence of mind not to be touched in anger. I've heard her tell the native wives at Fort Detroit to wait until their drunken husbands were asleep, then tie them up and beat them soundly with their iron frying pans. Stops the worst cases of wife beating."

"Ponthe and Beauty disagree about everything." Perish didn't meet her glance as he lifted his canoe to his shoulders. "That's why they live apart."

"What do they argue about?" Dorothy couldn't believe either member of the dignified couple could resort to pettiness.

"The Great Spirit." Perish looked at her then, a deep sadness in his eyes. "Ponthe doesn't believe in the spiritual world."

"But, you do."

"My vision was as real as you." His dimple winked at her.

"I told you the first day I met you that I doubt with nearly as much zeal as I believe." Dorothy hoped she could find someone to share her life, in spite of her lack of consistent faith.

"Ponthe taught me honesty is as important as faith is to God."

"I envy you," Dorothy said. "I don't remember my father."

"What does your mother tell you about him?"

"He preached about her faults in front of the entire congregation." It was important Perish not judge her mother. "Mother said she wasn't smart enough. He finally turned away from her in bed."

Perish shook his head. "We allow divorce."

"My father confessed her screams in childbirth had taken his manhood away."

"The coward," Perish said, then apologized. "Sorry, but she's the one who felt the pain."

"That's how we ended up at Fort Detroit." Dorothy stopped and accepted another drink of water. "I do enjoy the books." She shook her head in despair. "Bishop Pascal has forbidden Father Sebastian to allow me in his Jesuit library." An angry tear escaped. She brushed it aside. "Because of my doubts."

"I don't doubt my vision," Perish said. "I hope I'll be able to tell you some day.

Dorothy relaxed with a deep breath. She was important to him. Wasn't that almost a proposal? "When I'm family?"

He smiled but didn't say anything more on the subject.

"I had a great dream the day before we left," she said. "We've been too busy for me to tell you about it.

Perish matched his step to hers. "Tell me now."

Ponthe motioned for them to walk with him. Dorothy went to the shaded side of the up-turned canoe Ponthe was carrying while Perish, hauling his small canoe, maneuvered to the other side. Jimmy trailed four steps behind them with his hands above his head, holding onto the struts of Ponthe's over-turned canoe.

"You don't believe in dreams," Perish challenged his father's interest.

"I believe dreams." Ponthe adjusted the weight of the canoe. "They show all there is to say about the people dreaming them."

"What did my vision tell you?" Perish asked.

"That you're ready to look for a wife to start a family."

- 40 -

Dorothy hurried forward to keep up with Ponthe. He slowed his steps to match hers, which she appreciated. The exertion from the backpack was making her hair wet with sweat. She swiped at a fresh line of wetness near her ear with the back of her hand. "I dreamt of a cathedral of trees. What does that mean?"

"Tell me more," Ponthe said.

"There were trillium growing everywhere and the flowers were tinged with hues from the stained glass church windows."

"Have you seen stained glass windows?" Perish asked.

"Only in books," she admitted. "Oh, oh," she said, forgetting for a moment about the heavy load on her back. "There were books instead of people, and animals lying together in the aisles."

"You like to make peace." Ponthe smiled at her from under the rim of the canoe. "But you think you cause more strife than peace."

"Yes," Dorothy said. "That's disappointing. I believed the dream was heaven."

"To you," Ponthe touched her shoulder. "It is."

Dorothy knew he was serious. "So we dream reality with the magical elements we wish for?"

"Not always," Ponthe said. "I'm sure Bishop Pascal doesn't allow himself to remember his dreams."

"Just as well," Perish grumbled.

Ponthe stopped. "Here, you can carry the big canoe."

"Thank you father," Perish said, lowering the smaller canoe he and Dorothy had paddled in.

Jimmy sat down on the ground with his end of the supply canoe resting on his head.

Ponthe went on ahead, checking with each person in the line. When he reached Henry, he stopped and held up his hand. "Time to make camp." His loud command reached Perish and Dorothy. "We only have an hour until dark."

Dorothy hurried to set her pots cooking. No more time to dream of Perish and how it would be with her own family, living and playing together. She had to admit she was mostly interested in the playing part. She tried to concentrate. Had she salted the rabbit stew once or twice? Dorothy North wouldn't be a heavy name to carry.

* * *

Two days later, the travelers reached the Thames River crossing, where Ponthe had promised to meet his brother Hurons. Across the river, Dorothy counted seven natives. Added to the nine men on her side of the river, she wasn't sure she had enough coffee for another meal.

Ponthe came up to her as she stood looking down at her supplies. "We'll feed them once we cross."

"Their camp fires are waiting," she said, wearily packing the canoe.

"We all like boating rather than walking," Perish said.

Surprised at his voice so close behind her, Dorothy whirled around and the empty coffee pot fell out of the kettle, landing on his boot. Rather than stepping back Perish hung onto her shoulders as he jumped out of the way. They both spilled onto the grass.

Ponthe turned around from his chores and laughed at them. "When you two puppies stop your tomfoolery, we could start to cross."

"We weren't fooling around." Perish tried to reassemble his dignity, which only made Dorothy laugh.

"I'm sorry, I'm sorry." Dorothy helped Perish pick dusty leaves from his hair.

"Stop," he said.

The Bishop took a step in their direction, but Dasquorant blocked his way.

Dorothy dropped her arms, aware she was embarrassing Perish. "I am sorry." She motioned her head in the Bishop's direction. "When I'm overly tired, I usually drop things. Mother always says...."

The thought of her mother made her suddenly homesick. Uninvited tears spilled down her cheeks. She turned away so Perish couldn't see them.

Perish pleaded. "Don't cry."

Ponthe immediately appeared on her right with Dasquorant on her left. Both men scowled at Perish.

"Just because you're clumsy," Ponthe said, "you shouldn't make a woman cry."

Dasquorant stared down at Perish. "Clan Mother says words can hurt worse than blows."

"No, no." Dorothy moved directly in front of Perish to shield him from their misunderstanding. "I was thinking of my mother, and started to cry."

Perish's chin went up. "We're all tired, Father. Maybe we should rest here before crossing the river."

"My Huron brothers would not understand," Ponthe said.

"Impolite," Dasquorant agreed.

* * *

The travelers packed the canoes tightly and started to cross the river. The current was swifter than anticipated, bringing the group south of the Huron camp.

Dorothy was probably more exhausted than he was and he tried to paddle back up the river.

Dorothy didn't understand. She stood to call to the others to come back.

At the sound of her voice, Henry Holt stood up in Ponthe's canoe.

With his back turned, Perish didn't realize Dorothy had stood up and leaned to the other side just as she sat down, overturning the canoe. As Perish went over, he remembered...Dorothy couldn't swim. When he reached her, she clung to his body, pulling him under. He doubled up his fist and struck her on the jaw, then pulled her limp, floating body to shore.

Matthew and Thomas helped drag her up the bank. Perish recognized his father's Huron brothers.

"Ponthe wouldn't like you hitting a woman," Matthew said.

"She was dragging him under," Thomas countered.

Dorothy was coming around. "Did I drown?"

"Almost." Perish smiled in relief. "You are thoroughly wet."

Ponthe and the treaty party arrived on foot. They were carrying Perish's canoe along with their own two. Henry had a blanket wrapped around his shoulders.

"I fell in, too," he said cheerfully, as if it were a new game.

Dasquorant didn't appear any happier with Perish. "Why did they stand up?"

"I thought you didn't see us turn around," Dorothy said.

Dasquorant looked down at her. "Lucky Perish knew how to handle a struggling swimmer."

"Or you both could have drowned." Ponthe said.

"I saw you hit her." Bishop Pascal put in his two cents before being hustled off between Crane and Flat Belly.

Dorothy rubbed her chin and looked up at Perish. "You struck me?"

Ponthe laughed. "Worse than that, you'll catch a chill unless we get that dress off of you."

Dorothy fainted.

Perish looked at his father. "Now what do we do?"

"Take her into my tent." John Hicks, another Huron, said.

Perish recognized all seven of the men, milling about his unconscious friend. Five had been in Washington: George Punch, War Pole, Chief Honor, and T. Aruntue, who was sometimes called Between the Logs.

Henry and Lieutenant Cass brought Dorothy's belongings to John Hicks' tent.

"You should teach that girl not to stand up in a canoe," Jimmy Sweetwater shook his head in dismay. "Now, who's going to cook for us?"

Aruntue spoke. "Eat with us this evening. We can smoke and then talk in the morning, after we know the white girl is healthy."

* * *

Inside the tent, Dorothy hung her head, watching as river water dripped from the fringe hem of her buckskin dress into the tops of her muddy boots.

"I'll turn my back, and you hand me your dress," Ponthe said.

Dorothy did as she was told. She was surprised at herself for not being able to stop weeping. Fainting was new to her, too. "I'm a strong woman," she said more to herself than to Ponthe.

"Of course you are." Ponthe said, quietly. "Dorothy, are you sixteen yet?"

"In May," she said. "Why?"

Ponthe faced the entrance of the tent. He handed her a soft red blanket behind his back. "I'm sorry there are no women in the camp to talk to you."

"I like you," Dorothy said in all honesty. "Mother said to trust you."

"You get warm under the blanket," Ponthe said, with his back still turned away. "Throw me your clothes. We'll hang them outside. I'm going to come back with a cup of coffee. We need to talk."

After shedding her wet clothes and tossing them toward the tent's entrance, Dorothy wrapped herself from shoulder to toe in the large blanket, before asking, "Ponthe, did I do something wrong?"

"No." Ponthe turned and touched the top of her wet head, twice. "Be back with coffee."

Dorothy huddled under the blanket, hugging her knees to her chest. What did Ponthe need to talk to her about? Maybe he didn't want her to talk to Perish anymore. Worse, maybe he didn't approve of them as a couple...for the future. What would she do? For the rest of the trip? For the rest of her life? She tried to muffle her sobs. Her life was ruined, now. Her crying rose in volume.

She'd made Perish lose face in front of the others. Now his father wouldn't let her near him again. She'd end up a pariah, an outcast, like the Bishop. Combing out her wet hair, Dorothy regained some of her composure by trying to forgive herself for her hating the horrible Bishop. He reminded her of a slimy bug. That's probably how Ponthe viewed her, untouchable. She couldn't contain her loud sobs for another moment.

Maybe the Lord was getting even with her for causing the Bishop to be such an evil person. Now Ponthe would have her shunned.

Chapter Five

Ontario Peninsula

When Ponthe first came out of John Hicks' tent, Perish watched him move Dorothy's clothing bag inside. Perish could hear Dorothy's sobbing increase in volume. Why was she so upset? She was surely unhurt and nothing terrible had happened. Was she missing her mother? Would they need to send her home? If she was sent back to Fort Detroit, he decided he would go with her.

Ponthe hit him on the chest to get his attention. "Hang this dress up to dry while we still have daylight."

Perish took the buckskin dress his mother had made for Dorothy. Half in a daze, he found a branch to hang the damp dress over. As he shook out the garment, Dorothy's soaked pantaloons fell to the ground. Perish looked around to see if anyone noticed. If they had, they had all turned their backs to him. He hung up the snowy white garment, noticing the blue butterflies embroidered on the hem of each leg.

A whimsical girl, she was. How she would fare in a native's life? Their trip would answer that question. At least, she hadn't asked to be taken home. Would he ever be man enough to feed six children? Dorothy had mentioned the number to the Seneca Clan Mother, Whipping Stick. And, what about the influence of the Dominican nuns? Bishop Pascal had promised her mother Dorothy would be educated in Washington after the trip. Would Dorothy come back to him then, or would she find a brighter future for herself in the white man's world? He looked at his hands. White hands. What could he do to win her over?

Perish stopped moping about and went in search of coffee supplies. He thanked the Lord. Dorothy was alive and within reach for nine months.

The sun was setting behind them, letting orange traces color the clouds opposite the camp, as well as the river they had dumped Dorothy in. He'd need to make sure no other accident befell this young woman, who his vision guide promised to let him father generations with. Perish wondered if he'd be able to persuade

Dorothy she was meant for him. The trip ahead was long enough. Could he convince her, and himself, he could provide for all her needs…and those of the six children she wanted?

"Nine months," Perish said aloud, then turned to Thomas and Matthew. "Do you have coffee I could borrow?"

"Of course." Thomas folded himself down beside the low burning campfire.

Matthew poured a cup of coffee for Perish from the pot sitting next to the fire. "Not nine months' worth." He sat next to his brother.

Perish took a sip from the cup. "Dorothy said we were running low." Perish wished his father could help barter as he joined his uncles. "We haven't brought along many trade items."

"Ponthe is our brother," Thomas, the younger, said.

"Gifts are not for trading." Matthew pointed to a large bag of coffee among a pile of supplies near the campfire. "You need to keep it dryer than your powder."

Perish laughed. "I don't think Dorothy will stand up in my canoe again."

The seven Hurons and eight of the nine travelers laughed, too.

* * *

Dorothy could hear them. She stopped sobbing. When Ponthe had re-entered the tent with a cup of coffee, she spoke as quietly as she could. "You don't want me to talk to Perish, do you? That's what you're going to tell me. I'm too white for his life? I'm not. I love it outside. I would need a few books. You know I work hard."

Ponthe held up his hand for quiet. "None of that now." He handed her the cup of coffee. "Drink, and then I'll tell you what we need to talk about. It's not Perish."

Dorothy drank as much as she could of the strong brew. Not wanting to waste the coffee, she handed to cup to Ponthe. "Can you finish the rest?"

He did in a gulp. "Your mother will need to know I spoke to you so personally."

She couldn't imagine what he wanted to say. Ponthe looked inside the empty cup as if searching for the right words. She tried to put him at ease. "Mother likes you."

Ponthe didn't raise his eyes. "I need to make sure you understand…about your body getting ready to make babies…the bleeding."

"Oh yes," Dorothy sighed with relief. "I've got all I need with me. I'm a little late. I've been a woman for two years, almost."

"I've observed you and Perish very closely." Ponthe sat himself and the empty cup on the rough blanket rug carpeting the tent. Ponthe traced signs into the carpet's nap. "You haven't acted as man and wife?"

Dorothy's eyes seem glued open by the coffee or the subject. "No, Ponthe." She kept her chin up. "We do kiss." Then she lowered her eyes, remembering all the sensations the kiss had engendered. "I like kissing Perish. I like Perish, a lot."

"I know," Ponthe smiled slightly. "It's the trip," he coughed and folded his arms. "I'm afraid. The hard work has told your body not to work."

"I work hard," Dorothy objected. Then she understood, and shook her head.

"Beauty often traveled with me before I brought Perish to her. There were times we hoped a baby was coming because her body stopped its monthly functioning." Ponthe let out a long breath. "She worked as hard as I did on the trail."

Dorothy felt like weeping loudly, all over again. "I want children. Does this mean I'll never have any children like you and Beauty?"

"No, no." Ponthe moved closer and hugged her to his side. "But when women are on a strenuous trip, like this one, they sometimes stop following the moon's cycles."

Dorothy wasn't sure she should believe him.

"I wouldn't lie to you."

"I know." Dorothy tried to stop her unwanted tears.

"Beauty wept a great deal, too. Like you, now." Ponthe cursed in the Iroquois language.

Dorothy's tears flowed heavier at the thought of Perish's kiss at the sight of the rainbow. "At rainbows?" she asked.

Ponthe nodded. "One time a baby rabbit ran across our path and we had to sit for hours until she could stop her tears."

Somehow that helped, another woman -- someone she admired -- had lost control. "I don't remember speaking to my father." She wiped her face with the soft blanket. "I guess you're the closest I ever had to a father. Ponthe," she had to ask. "Why does Perish smell like juniper?"

A short laugh of relief shook Ponthe. "The evergreen berry. He has a habit of crushing them with his fingernail. We began giving him the berries strung together, when he was a babe. Babies like something to hold onto. I'll find you some." Ponthe patted her back, "And Dorothy if you accept Perish's way of life or he accepts yours, both Beauty and I would be happy for you."

He left the tent after touching her forehead with his thumb.

Mercy, she wasn't even sixteen and she might have already met her future husband and father-in-law. And, she didn't have to worry about hiding her time of month. A big smile spread across Dorothy's face, before she leaned over and fell asleep.

* * *

In the morning, Perish found someone had stolen Dorothy's pantaloons during the night. "It could not have been a raccoon," he told his father.

"Let's not worry her," Ponthe said. "If she asks, I'll come up with something. I know she brought extras. It's a good thing the wind kept up all night to dry the buckskin."

"It's a little stiff." Dorothy laughed as she came out of John Hicks' tent. She stood with her arms outstretched like a scarecrow.

Ponthe and Perish laughed at her and pushed her arms down to her sides.

"Ponthe's brothers have given us enough coffee for the entire trip," Perish said, knowing Dorothy was concerned about her dwindling supply.

"We can keep some of the coffee beans in cans?" she asked Ponthe.

"No," Ponthe said. "We'll put them in two bags instead of one. It will have to do."

"If they get wet," Dorothy said. "I can dry them during the night."

"Planning to jump back in the river?" Henry pushed at her shoulder.

"Do you know how to swim?" she asked the young boy, envious of the skill.

Henry pointed at the three Hurons approaching. Chief Honor, War Pole, and George Punch joined the group. "War Pole gave me a black arrowhead."

George Punch placed his hand on Henry's head. "I made water wings for my children to wear when they learned to swim."

"Water wings?" Dorothy moved the coffee pot to a safe place in the fire. "How do you make them?"

"Do you use boar bladders?" Perish asked.

Dorothy put her hands on her hips. "If you knew about them, why didn't I have any?"

"He wanted to save you." Jimmy Sweetwater tried to wrestle the taller Perish to the ground.

Ponthe got their attention with a loud clap. "After we finish the cornbread, we need to speak about the treaty."

Perish and Jimmy strung up the tablecloth map again.

"We have 190 people to feed," John Hicks said.

"We Hurons are covered in Article One of the treaty," Ponthe said. "When we cede the Wyandott land given to us in the Greenville Treaty, President Monroe promises us different sections." Ponthe shaded in part of the tablecloth with a brush dipped in oil and paprika.

Perish had made the brush for his father. Before using the paprika, he convinced Dorothy that the natives didn't find the mild spice of paprika as savory as she did.

Ponthe continued, "Beginning at a point on the northern shore of Lake Erie, where the Indian boundary intersects the same, between the mouth of Sandusky Bay and the mouth of the Portage River, running south to the line established in the Greenville Treaty, which runs from the crossing place above Fort Lawrence to Loramie's store; then west to the line at the eastern end of the reserve at Loramie's store; then with the line north and west, to the northwestern corner, then to the north western reserve on the St. Mary's River, at the head of the waters, then east to the western bank of the river, then down on the western bank to the reserve at Fort Wayne."

Mathew interrupted. "That's too complicated for any settler to remember.

"Even us," Thomas added.

Ponthe only nodded. "Let me finish. Then, we'll discuss the problems."

* * *

Dorothy tried to be invisible, re-filling coffee cups, now that she didn't have to worry about her supply. She attempted to fill Bishop Pascal's cup, but Dasquorant stepped between them.

He took the Bishop's cup from his hand and held it out for Dorothy to fill.

Dorothy kept her eyes lowered. She wanted to forgive the Bishop so that everyone would stop demeaning the poor old man.

"Pity is never helpful," Dasquorant whispered to her before she moved on to the next empty cup. "Ask Perish about Atotarho."

Ponthe's voice held a sad tone as he continued the treaty term's description, "...northerly to the banks of the Maumee River of Lake Erie, down the north bank to the western line of land ceded to the government by the Detroit Treaty, then south to the middle of the river, opposite the mouth of the Great Au Glaze; then down and easterly with the lines of tract ceded so that a south line will strike the place of beginning."

"You can hunt and make sugar on all the land." Lieutenant Cass tried to sweeten the bitter pie. "Article 15 says Indian lands will not be taxed."

War Pole drew his finger down the middle of the Maumee River. "Hard to fish on only one side of a river."

No one laughed.

"Where is this line?" George Punch asked about a line crossing an empty plane.

Chief Honor nearly put his nose on the tablecloth. "Is that where the old trace crosses?"

Ponthe shrugged. "There's more." He consulted a pack of papers tied up in a stiff leather pouch.

Bishop Pascal drew nearer.

Ponthe nodded in his direction. "Three sections of 640 acres each have been allotted for the missionary and the schools. Another section is provided for mechanics, a sawmill, blacksmith shop, and agent's trading post. The agent assigned to the post will establish taverns and ferries."

Perish motioned for the Huron members to sit down. Ponthe looked more tired than Dorothy remembered. She would be careful not to solicit any need for his concern.

"For the seven of you who will attend the conference at the Maumee River Rapids, two sections each will be given to: War Pole,

Chief Honor, Between the Logs, John Hicks, George Punch, Thomas, and Matthew."

"And you, brother?"

Ponthe shook his head no. "I'll stay with Beauty on the Raisin River now that we are getting older."

She wouldn't ask, but Dorothy wondered if Perish would receive a grant of land. He didn't seem concerned as he hunkered down, carving on a stone pipe. "Will they have enough land to feed so many?"

Perish perked up. "A shaman will bless their best fisherman as they lay on their backs. He'll remind them, and the fish, that Hurons don't burn fish bones. They ask the fish to kindly allow themselves to be taken."

Dorothy loved his voice. The low tones sent nice feelings all through her as she knelt alongside him.

"They keep their seines close to the weirs they build."

"Nets?"

"And underwater cages."

The fire was extinguished and the treaty map stowed away. Everyone shouldered their share of the supplies. The canoes would be lifted over their heads before they headed north.

George Punch walked next to Henry. As they passed her, Dorothy listened into their conversation.

"You lost your dice?" George asked.

"In the river," Henry said. "The toad probably made it. He wasn't in my pocket when I they pulled me out."

"I have these," George said, giving Henry a handful of something.

Dorothy's curiosity got the best of her. "Let me see," she called to the two.

Henry hurried back. "Look, look!" He held his hand out.

All Dorothy found were, "Black and white beans?"

"You throw and count them," George explained.

"To gamble with. Same as dice," Henry said. "Thanks. Do you want my buttons?"

Dorothy couldn't imagine what George Punch could do with four buttons.

"My wife will be pleased," George said.

"Where will you next camp?" Matthew and Thomas closed in on Ponthe. "Will we see you before the powwow at Maumee Rapids?" Dorothy was busy tighting the straps on her pack and noticed she couldn't distinguish between the voices of the two brothers.

"Fort Mackinac is next," Ponthe said. "I hope the Ottawa will be as agreeable to the treaty as you, my brothers. Henry assures me he knows sign language." The Hurons shook their heads, unsure about that piece of news. Ponthe nodded. "Then the Delaware, Potawatomi, Shawnee, and Chippewa."

"Who knows Chippewa?" Matthew asked.

"Jimmy Sweetwater," Ponthe said.

"Watch they don't ply him with liquor," Chief Honor cautioned.

John Hicks approached the group with a roll of canvas under his arm. "Ponthe, Dorothy Evans needs her own tent. Please take this smelly army thing. I've been carrying it around since the war."

"We'll put the tent to good use." Lieutenant Cass accepted the gift for Dorothy.

Ponthe waved to Matthew and Thomas as they departed the Huron camp. "I'll stop at the Mississippi to leave gifts for you."

Dorothy wanted to talk to Perish about his father's visit to John Hicks' tent, but Dasquorant followed them in the portage line.

"Who is Atotarho?" Dorothy asked, instead

"I'll take the canoe for a while." Dasquorant switched loads with Parish, as if he acknowledged the subject of Atotarho would impair him.

Dorothy noticed Perish considered the topic personal enough to let the tall Seneca walk ahead, out of earshot, before he told her, "Atotarho is a demonic shaman whose evil infected his own being to the point that snakes coiled around his brow."

"Mercy," Dorothy said. "Or in his brain? Dasquorant thinks Bishop Pascal is Atotarho."

"Could be," Perish said.

Dorothy wondered if she'd ever be able to discuss the personal subjects Ponthe and she covered in the tent. Perhaps someday, when they were family. Instead, she asked, "Will you tell me about when you met President Monroe, while we hike?"

Chapter Six

Ontario Peninsula

"Last summer," Perish began telling Dorothy about his trip, trying to remember every detail, "in Washington DC, the White House honor guards let me pass without so much as a comment, but they crossed their guns to bar Ponthe's entrance."

Dorothy gasped.

"I pushed their guns aside and told them. 'He's my father.' Ponthe only grinned and pulled on my knife sheath. It was identical to his. Beauty made the Iroquois beadwork. Ponthe embarrassed me by tugging at my blond braids. Even though the sun tans my skin nearly as dark as my father's, my hair bleaches lighter each summer."

"What was it like inside?" Dorothy's rapt attention opened Perish's memory.

"The ceiling inside the entrance of the great house seemed as high as the pines in northern Michigan. I tried to imagine the timber bracings under the painted walls." Perish laughed at himself. "Of course, my nervousness didn't come from the threat of a heavy ceiling."

"How many tribes were there?" Her quick mind knew which questions to ask...the important ones.

"All seven tribal leaders from the State of Ohio, Michigan Territory, Illinois, Indiana and New York States made the long trip south." Perish took his time listing them and their attributes to cover any information the Jesuit library might have omitted from Dorothy's education. "The Iroquois speaking tribes were present. Hurons trap furs throughout Michigan and Illinois. Seneca are the western gatekeepers from the old Iroquois nation. Delaware, from the last of the New York woodlands, carried the wooden Red Score clan histories of the wolf, turtle and turkey. The Iroquois tribes used sign language to communicate with the three Algonquin tongued tribes. The Potawatomi settled in the fields of the annihilated tribe of Illinois. The Shawnees, Tecumseh's bold brothers; and the Ottawa, Pontiac's descendants, were represented, too. The Chippewa, or

Ojibway, as the southwestern Hopi know the roaming traders, all sent delegates."

"Then you won't be meeting complete strangers on the trip?" Dorothy touched his arm as she skipped ahead to look directly at him.

Perish smiled at his vision mate, Dorothy, incarnate before him. Life was not one long tax of his energies. The Great Spirit deemed to reward his search for truth with this lovely girl-woman cavorting before him. He hoped his story of Washington didn't seem prideful to her. "We stood in our most festive trappings, ready to meet the Great White Father in person. Faces of grim old white men stared at us from framed paintings. White statues of robed people perched on columns as high as a man's chest. Intricate tile work covered the floor. White men gathered great fortunes to amass all those artifacts."

"Their greed has no bounds," Dorothy said.

Perish nodded in agreement. "I compared the room's grandeur to our modest wampum tributes, recalling the deeds of tribal heroes. The hallowed presents for the Great White Father would be misunderstood. For too long natives have used the colorful beadwork to barter for goods."

Dorothy agreed. "Every book, well almost every one in Father Sebastian's library, has more than one story about the corruption, the evilness, and the untrustworthy qualities of white men. I'm convinced I should live in pure nature."

"Without books?" Perish knew the answer.

"I might need a few," Dorothy admitted. "Tell me more about the meeting."

"I remember the coldness of the marble floor crept through the soles of my boots. I certainly missed Mother's fresh smelling wigwam. Kdahoi, or Beauty, knows when my thoughts turn to her. Beauty is a shaman and member of the Midewiwin Society. That's why she lives alone, away from her village. Even now, she keeps a string of awareness tied to me, and to all those she loves...even Ponthe who never ceases to argue with her."

Dorothy nodded her head. "You told me they don't live together."

Perish continued, "I first believed Ponthe traveled too much to claim one place as home. But he owns a log cabin near the Portage

Lake. I finally realized Beauty's Potawatomi beliefs are at odds with my adopted Huron father's."

"How are they different?"

"Ponthe refuses to recognize spiritual powers. Even when he speaks reverently about the Iroquois Great Spirit, Orenda, Ponthe refers to reality's sway in earthly matters. The first argument I remember concerned my adoption. Beauty swears she'd made my cradle board weeks before our friend the French voyager, Ed Renault, arrived with the news of Ponthe's burden. Me that is. Ponthe didn't believe her. 'It doesn't matter,' Ponthe always says and then adds, 'I knew the babe had a green-eyed, beautiful mother waiting for him.'"

"Was Clan Mother right?" Dorothy asked. "She said your real mother was white, but not your father."

"I wonder how she knows?" Perish stopped walking. Dorothy waited for him to continue. Perish resumed their trek north. "It's getting colder, isn't it?"

"As long as I keep walking, I don't notice; but I think you're right. The rain looks an hour away. Should you ask Ponthe, if we should stop; so I can cook?"

"There's no shelter near," Perish said as he quickened his steps. "We'll talk more later."

Dorothy laughed, keeping up with him. "You have an entire year to tell me about Washington."

* * *

On Lake Huron

The rain started falling in earnest when all three canoes were underway north on Lake Huron. The natives used blankets to cover themselves. Dorothy's dress had a hood attached. Was it designed to carry a papoose? She used her blanket for her shoulders, wrapping the ends of the blanket tightly under her knees.

Bishop Pascal declined to accept a blanket even after he was thoroughly soaked. Dorothy knew his belief system included the tenet of self-flagellation used to return his soul to God's grace.

Dorothy once put pebbles in her slippers to release the suffering souls from Purgatory. But the pain was too much for her. The damned were on their own, as far as she was concerned. She intuitively knew suffering was not a punishment from God. An eternal creator would only want to be loved. Enough sacrifice was already made once by Jesus, if one believed the scriptures.

The air got cooler with each stroke of Perish's paddle. Finally the rain turned to a heavy, wet snow. When the blizzard hindered their vision, Ponthe called a halt.

* * *

An overhanging cliff on the Michigan shore beckoned to the exhausted crew. Perish and Henry found enough drift wood to make a roaring fire. The wind whipped sparks up to the snow swirling off the cliff above them. The men positioned the smaller canoes to hold up the larger one against the wall of the cliff. They provided a cramped shelter for the nine men. John Hicks' army tent was set up for Dorothy.

The wind competed with the raging fire. They stuffed their supplies into the openings around the canoes.

As snow continued to fall, Dorothy labored over the cornbread, which decided to burn over the roaring fire. She also provided dried fish and coffee to refresh the group's spirits.

Bishop Pascal's coughing echoed through the night.

Perish crept into Dorothy's tent. "Are you sleeping?" he whispered.

Dorothy pulled him down so she could whisper close to his ear. "I can't sleep with all that coughing."

Perish inserted himself, fully clothed, under her blanket. His back was to the tent opening. The cold had kept her from undressing, too. She couldn't see Perish's face. His lips found hers and he cradled her in his arms, just for a moment.

Then Perish leaned on one elbow. "Let me tell you the rest of the Washington story. We can't sleep anyway."

Dorothy agreed, wanting to still the storm running riot through her veins. "We need to keep our voices low."

"Ponthe introduced me to the tribes as his most honored son. Not one stranger in the tribes blinked at the title of acceptance for me. I wished my manhood rites had been completed before the trip. Then I might have held my head as high as my father's knowing the Great Spirit had honored me with a private vision. Pride kept me from asking each man in the room about the miracles in their visions. I expected to find meaning for my existence. I wanted to find why my soul felt alone around people and at one with nature."

Dorothy stroked Perish's hand. "I am the same."

Perish nodded, but continued his Washington story. "Double doors opened inside, across from the entrance, admitting a group of dark-suited interpreters. I recognized three of them: Army Lieutenant C. Louis Cass, Henry Jackson Holt, and Jimmy Sweetwater.

"As Ponthe started to make the formal introductions, an older black-suited man raised his hand in the air. 'We will pair each of you up with a sworn interpreter.' Then he rudely motioned for Ponthe to follow him. My father shrugged his shoulders at me and followed the man into the inner chambers. A great deal of confusion ensued."

"Why what happened?" Dorothy asked. She loved his soft voice. She could feel the warmth of Perish's breath on her ear and neck.

"The interpreters shouted in badly pronounced dialects, as if the natives were deaf. The group of Indians shook their heads in consternation. No one moved. After nearly twenty minutes of continuous din, Ponthe returned to the entrance hall with an older man in tow. My father quietly introduce the tribal leaders to their chosen interpreters, apologizing to each for their garbled speech.

"When the black-suited man again tried to lead Ponthe into the inner rooms, Ponthe motioned for the Delaware representatives, the grandfather tribe, to lead the way for the Iroquois. Perish followed his father's Huron brothers, noting the Seneca in matching clothes. The Algonquin tribes of the Ottawa, the Potawatomi with their cleft chins and the proud Shawnee came next. The independent Chippewa traders followed in some disarray."

Parish gently stroked Dorothy's long hair. The comfort reminded her of her mother brushing out her hair before bedtime. She pinched herself, fighting sleep, trying to hear every word of Perish's.

"President Monroe stood behind a podium which blocked a long hallway. He spoke soft, welcoming sentences, which the interpreters whispered to their alert charges. The meeting was shorter than I anticipated. The tribal leaders were given no opportunity to speak."

"That's terrible," Dorothy whispered. She reached up and cupped Perish's jaw with her left hand, feeling the vibrations of his voice as his jaw moved.

"Ponthe broke rank. A flurry of guards and male secretaries attempted to intervene. But, Ponthe handed President Monroe a roll of birch-bark. Wampum strings from each of the assembled tribes were tied to its seals. Unperturbed by the uproar around him, Ponthe spoke. 'We have rolled our words into one bundle.'

"The President graciously bowed to Ponthe before his minions hustled the great man away from the speaker's stand and down the echoing hall. We were then ushered out to a side lawn where tables were laden with enough food for the road home. Several of us pushed the food under our shirts.

"I breathed in deeply of the fresh air after the stale, dank air of the White House. The sun was pleasant on my shoulders, and the strange food filled my stomach. I wanted my father to choose a shade tree to sit under before a nap overwhelmed me."

Dorothy tried to focus in the dark tent. Was Perish fighting sleep as much as she was?

But he kept at his unbroken story, "Ponthe ignored the beating sun. He stood next to the nearly empty food table with the tribal leaders who took polite turns to speak with him.

"I daydreamed about becoming the next hero of the Indian Nation. I moved closer to my father to hear his words. Ponthe was drawing on the cloth covering the food table. With a piece of charcoal he had outlined the Lakes of Erie, Ontario, Huron, Superior, and Michigan. As he drew the Mississippi and Ohio River lines, Ponthe described where the white man would allow land for the Indian Reservations."

Dorothy recognized the treaty map Ponthe had shown the Seneca Clan Mother, Whipping Stick.

"'Old treaties are no longer good.' My father's voice was sad. 'You know the Americans are like their old chiefs, the English. Only land will appease them. We can mourn the French who only killed our game, but we must be as tame as a caged bear now. Our families need to eat and this is where the white men will allow us to live. Old land grants have to be handed back, and hopefully our grandchildren,' Ponthe caught my eye and lowered his voice, 'will be able to depend on Monroe's words.'

"Soon, another group of white men entered the garden, headed for the table. With a nod to Ponthe, I swept the tablecloth into a tight bundle and into my satchel.

"The officials issued orders to the interpreters, who then guided their charges along the boardwalks of several streets to another meeting hall. In a windowless room, Secretary John Quincy Adams, Jr. commanded one person from each tribe sit down at his long conference table.

"Outside the meeting room, the rejected natives leaned against the wood paneling. I kept my ears open as I inched down the hall as nonchalantly as I could. At an open door I heard three men arguing.

"'I didn't pave Monroe's way to the presidency to be told no at my first expansion idea.' The first speaker's old voice sounded like a viper's whisper.

"'The Hudson River connection to the Erie Canal will open up the West,' a second compatriot boasted.

"The third man diplomatically kept the conversation on neutral terms. 'Of course, the President wants to hear your plans. The Army has advised us the area is not peaceful enough from the last war to encourage more settlers.'

"The loud one swore, before demanding, 'Let the Army get in there and wipe up the troublemakers.'

"'The President is asking Congress to ratify a treaty for that purpose,' the peaceful man tried to calm them.

"The first man hissed. 'Good, my investors will be pleased.'

"I sidled back to the group outside the Secretary of State's office to wait for my father. As the three men in the adjoining room exited past, I detected glints of gold watch chains and rings. Wealth was evident."

Dorothy was convinced she would never sleep again. She let Perish know whose side she was on. "Like ants following honey trails, opening Braddock's wagon trail from Virginia to Fort Pitt, and Forbes' longer military access from Philadelphia allowed greedy land speculators to rob you of your lands. I read in Father Sebastian's books that King George III's Proclamation Line along the Alleghenies was meant to halt expansion into Indian Territory. The advancing horde of settlers never paused. The Wilderness Road through the Cumberland Gap brought more followers of Daniel Boone to the Old Northwest."

Perish added, "Neither Pontiac nor Tecumseh prevailed against the onslaught of families determined to become landowners.

Acceptance of the proposed treaty is a stopgap measure against the ultimate rule of the whites."

Dorothy's bowed her head.

Perish kissed held her hand. "When we retired to our hotel room that evening, Ponthe laid down on his bed and stared at the ceiling. He asked me what I thought of the Great White Father. 'A sad man. The weight of power has burdened his heart.'"

"Ponthe continued to stare at the ceiling. 'I like the sky better.'"

"I asked him how men breathed in their closed structures. Across the street curtains fluttered in the afternoon breeze."

"You were never in a whiteman's house, before?" Dorothy asked.

Perish shook his head. "'The windows slide up,' Ponthe told me. I opened all the windows. Most of the rain stayed out. Ponthe asked me, 'Did you listen to the Americans while I was closeted?' I told him what I had heard. At first, Ponthe sat up, then his shoulders slumped. He told me he'd promised to take a Jesuit Bishop to Fort Detroit."

"Bishop Pascal." Dorothy cringed.

"I think I said it wouldn't be an easy trip for a Bishop. 'Or his camp-mates.' Ponthe laughed, then he sobered. He told me, 'Your ears do you justice. You found valuable answers.'

"I told him I wished I had a better map of where the canal would run. 'It wouldn't help, Hehawalk,' my father said. He used the childish endearment to ease my discomfort. 'We have no bargaining tools. They'll put the canal where the Army Engineers tell them.'"

Dorothy coughed. "I know the 1795 Greenville Treaty and the 1807 Detroit Treaty were both walked on by avaricious settlers. They want all the land. Worse, they want Indians to disappear. They don't fear violence. Their greed for land and more land is insatiable. White fingers can't grab enough."

* * *

Perish considered his un-tanned palms. He was glad it was dark enough in the tent. Dorothy didn't see the flush of shame spreading from his neck to his hairline. "In Washington, my father told me, 'The heart is where life starts to mean anything, not the skin.'"

Dorothy kissed the palm of Perish's hand, letting him feel the tears on her face.

"Ponthe told me, 'Trust me, you're heart is true. The Great Spirit will not desert you. The rest of humanity's fate is unsettled.'"

Perish hoped his heart was strong enough to deny his white blood. All the wealth of the world seemed destined for white hands at the expense of the people he loved. It would take courage to survive in the future. If Cornplanter, Pontiac, and Tecumseh couldn't hold the settlers back, how could he?

"I felt a great sadness. The air seemed heavy in the room. I knew why alcohol so readily seeped into Jimmy Sweetwater's life. A momentary respite from reality is tempting. Then I felt Beauty's fingertip on the ridge between my nose and upper lip. 'Never,' her spirit whispered to me, 'Never.'"

Whenever Ponthe or Beauty were with him, Perish could forget for a moment he was of the same blood as the white men he needed to fight against...the same blood as Dorothy. He wanted Dorothy to give birth to his children. What was he doing?

A gust of wind startled the couple.

Ponthe stood outside. "Perish, help Dorothy move under the shelter. We need to put the Bishop in here."

"We weren't...," Perish started.

"Hurry," was the only word Ponthe uttered.

* * *

Dorothy unwrapped her blankets and donned her long, winter coat, lined with beaver pelts. The moon was high and the snow had stopped falling. She found Ponthe propped up against the wall of the cliff. His blanket was around the Bishop's shaking shoulders.

"My tent is ready," Dorothy offered.

Ponthe agreed. "His fever is high."

Crane and Flat Belly carried the uncomplaining Bishop into Dorothy's tent.

"He won't let us undress him," Crane said as he and Flat Belly crawled out of the small tent.

"Perhaps he'll sweat the fever out," Henry called sleepily.

Ponthe made room for Dorothy to bed down between the curve of the small canoe bottom and himself.

The Bishop's coughing stopped. Under the roof of the large canoe, eight men and one woman, wrapped neatly side by side against the storm, dozed off in the blessed stillness.

* * *

Bishop Pascal could smell Dorothy's familiar scent. He pulled up his cassock and fingered the blue butterflies on her pantaloons that he wore. Crazy, he told himself, to derive such hedonist pleasure from wearing a young girl's clothing. The thought of the material touching her made his mouth water. He was in Dorothy's tent, and he imagined her touching him.

Bishop Pascal crept out of the tent.

He headed north. He'd heard people describe the cliffs at Copper Harbor. He could have used the ledge high above their heads but he wanted to be as far away as possible from anyone who knew him. Maybe his body would be washed away after he jumped. Then no one would know about his warped sin. Except for the all-seeing Creator. Clan Mother was right; his soul was as twisted as a snake coiled against him.

* * *

Ponthe discovered the empty tent at daybreak. The snow had melted during the night and no tracks were found to follow. When Dorothy packed up her belongings, she noticed the Bishop had left his Bible. She brought it to Ponthe. "I'll carry the book back for Father Sebastian."

Lieutenant Cass held out his hand. "You have enough to concern yourself with. Let me keep it safe."

Ponthe nodded and Dorothy reluctantly gave him the only book in camp. "Could I read it when we have time?"

"We could take turns reading to the men," Lieutenant Cass said.

Dorothy agreed with a smile, but she wasn't sure she wanted to read to the others. What if she hurt their feelings by some of the dictates? She was glad to have the Bible available to her. The Psalms held such beauty.

Dasquorant appeared to be the most concerned about who would be blamed for the Bishop's loss. "How will we explain we didn't search for him?"

Lieutenant Cass tried to calm everyone. "No one is accusing anyone of foul play."

"Yet...." Ponthe pondered. "No one except the Huron and the Seneca know that Bishop Pascal left Fort Detroit with us."

Lieutenant Cass concurred. "He won't be mentioned again. When we get back to Fort Detroit, they'll think he went from Fort Meigs to Philadelphia. Anything could have happened to him by the time his Baltimore diocese eventually makes inquiries. The Lord will handle the problem."

Dasquorant shook his head. "I'm heading south. I can shoulder the blame."

"We can't spare a canoe," Ponthe tried to reason with him.

"I need to move," Dasquorant said. "The canoes restrict my limbs."

"Let him go, Ponthe." Crane turned his long neck from one side to the other.

Flat Belly bowed. "The Plains have called him in his sleep."

"Is that true, Dasquorant?" Ponthe reached up to lay a comforting hand on the giant's shoulder. "Have you dreamt the horse dream again?"

Dasquorant nodded. "A dwarf caressed my knees, but this time many men chased me."

Dorothy was surprised to hear herself say, "Don't leave us." Noticing Perish's attention, she added "How will we explain to Whipping Stick?"

Dasquorant came close and looked down at her. "Tell my Clan Mother, she was right. The trail calls my feet."

"You realize," Ponthe said in a gentle tone, "You will be considered outside the law."

"I doubt anyone will practice murder on me," Dasquorant said.

Dorothy recognized the term. It meant any native could kill him without punishment in the native world. "But you're innocent of any wrong doing."

"White men will have to blame someone," Dasquorant said. With only a few supplies and Henry's tin of matches, Dasquorant headed inland and southwest.

Chapter Seven

Fort Mackinac

For the remaining travelers, the trip to Mackinac was more difficult, even though no more snow fell and no portages were needed. They embarked at Clark Point to cross Lake Huron with Lieutenant Cass and Crane manning one side of the large canoe. Flat Belly, Jimmy, and Henry paddled on the other side. Losing two men, Dasquorant and the Bishop, meant each remaining man or boy had to work harder.

On the storm-free lake, Dorothy learned to paddle efficiently with Perish. Nevertheless, her arms ached when she cooked at the Port Austin campsite. That evening they enjoyed roast duck. Dorothy carefully saved the fat drippings.

When they crossed Thunder Bay and gained North Point's beach, Dorothy sent Jimmy and Henry off to forage for berries. They came back with pockets full of wild crab apples. So, after boiling the peeled apples with most of her sugar, Dorothy used the duck's fat and flour to bake a one-crust apple pie in the frying pan.

Perish had helped her position a rock at a slant in the fire pit. Under the rock, Dorothy placed the stew kettle on its side and inserted the pie, using the pot's lid as the door to the makeshift oven. They heaped burning wood on the top and at the sides and hoped for the best. The resulting pie's aroma made all of them hungry.

"You're a better cook than your mother," Crane said.

"Don't mention her mother," Flat Belly said, wolfing down his share of the pie in two gulps. "The memory makes her cry."

"I'm not crying," Dorothy defended herself. "But my mother does make a better crust."

Ponthe laughed. "If you tell Beauty, I'll switch your hide; but I've never tasted better."

Henry and Lieutenant Cass began to sing a ditty. "Can she bake a cherry pie, Perish boy, Perish boy?"

Perish and Jimmy Sweetwater took up the refrain, "She can bake an apple pie quick as a cat can wink its eye."

Crane and Flat Belly surprisingly knew the song, too. "She's a young thing but did leave her mother."

Dorothy busily scrubbed out the empty pans to hide the tears swelling in her eyes.

"Bed down," Ponthe instructed. "Save your energy for the last long trip to Fort Mackinac."

In her tent, Dorothy rubbed her arms. She was happy even though the song had touched her homesickness. Proved she could bake out in the wild, she had. As she lay quietly, she imagined some future when Perish would lay beside her, stroke her hair, breathe on her cheek, kiss her. She entered a deep, long and peaceful slumber. A gnat, moving near her hairline woke her. Dorothy swatted at the nuisance. Then a soft breeze swept her face.

Perish kissed her mouth.

Dorothy sat up knocking heads with him. "What are you doing here?"

"Seducing my bride-to-be," he said.

"Oh no," she whispered, hanging onto his neck with both hands. "First, tell me your manhood-rite dream vision."

Perish slipped under her blanket covering. Then, he told her a bit of the dream. "It was you. I saw you in the dress that Beauty made for you."

"But you'd already told Beauty about your dream before she made me the dress." Dorothy had let go of him. She sighed. "Didn't I have some kind of a message?"

His warm breath caressed the back of her neck as he cuddled against her back.

"Yes," he said. "You told me we would replenish generations."

Dorothy sighed. "Ponthe says I can't have children."

Perish moved away.

Dorothy sat up, pulling the blanket toward herself away from Perish. His chest was bare. "Oh," she said. "You're so beautiful." She nestled down next to him. "I haven't been a woman for two months now." Dorothy kissed him and looked into his eyes. "Ponthe says I'll be back to normal when I stop hiking."

Dorothy was so intent on Perish's reaction to her intimate revelations that she didn't hear footsteps in the harsh gravel of the shore.

Ponthe opened the tent flap. He looked concerned.

Dorothy pulled the blanket up to her neck.

Perish said, "We need to be together."

Ponthe hung his head. "Dorothy's mother would not approve."

"Nonsense," Dorothy said. "Mother only told me to stay away from the Bishop. She and Beauty both know I am interested in Perish. They knew before I left home." Dorothy's pride pushed away her modesty. "Neither of them wanted me to marry a stinky soldier."

Ponthe laughed. Perish joined in, a little sheepishly, Dorothy thought.

"This is not how you prove you're a man," Ponthe said to Perish.

"No." Perish said. "First, I need to know I can provide for six children." He wound an arm around Dorothy's waist.

"I have breakfast to make." Dorothy pushed Perish away.

Perish gave his father a puzzled look.

Ponthe howled with laughter. "Now it starts," he crowed.

* * *

After a cheerful breakfast, they moved out onto Lake Huron for their last part of the trip to Mackinac. They hugged the shoreline, which alternated between long stretches of white limestone pebbles and solid rock cliffs of granite with green and black basalt jutting over their heads. They could see hollowed out caverns high above the level of the lake. The shoreline was often marked by rugged cliffs, where the waves concentrated on pulverizing the jutting bare rocks and the rough cobbled beach into the sands of time.

Dorothy was awestruck. "I thought creation started somewhere near Jerusalem or the Euphrates. But this coast looks like our Creator resurrected it today, from under the great flood."

"Maybe the flood tipped up this end of the world," Perish said.

As they approached the northern tip of Thompson Island from its western side, Perish pointed to the white outlines of the military fort on the high plateau.

"Fort Mackinac," Flat Belly cried, "On Big Turtle Island."

Henry was in the lead canoe. To signal the turbaned Ottawa at the landing, he put his hand to the side of his mouth with one finger on his tongue. Then he hooked his index finger and moved his hand down to his stomach. Finally, he crossed his arms with the palms resting on his small chest.

The dozen or so Ottawa standing on the north shore looked at each other. Dorothy wasn't sure they understood Henry's message of peaceful talks. However, they did help pull the canoes ashore.

* * *

Fort Mackinac

Ponthe introduced the men he knew from their Washington meeting. "Pontiac, grandson of the War Chief."

Perish remembered the Ottawa in Washington. They were silent but friendly.

Ponthe continued, "McCarty, Inisquegin, leader of the Tusquagan Ottawa town, and your Peace Chief."

The Peace Chief was as warlike looking as the War Chief.

"The Dog, Tontagini or Tandaganie," Ponthe continued, "Twoatum, and Nowkesick."

Dorothy pulled at Perish's sleeve before she whispered. "Why do some people have three names and others only one?"

"Their status and dream names," Perish whispered back.

McCarty named nine more natives who then joined the crowd from Fort Mackinac. "Our shaman chief, Supay and his wife, Antonette."

Dorothy's attention seemed glued to Antonette, a native wife. Perish doubted if she even heard the rest of the seven names. He had to admit Dorothy and Antonette's clothing were not that dissimilar. Their hair was the same color, but instead of brown like Dorothy's, Antonette's eyes were big and black. The two young women exchange shy smiles.

Finally, McCarty turned to a trapper. "And this is Sawendebwas, Yellow Hair, or Peter Minor, the adopted son of Tandaganie, the Dog."

"Small boy makes signs that you want to eat until you're full," Yellow Hair said.

"What?" Ponthe said. "Excuse me for believing he knew sign language. We want to talk to you again about the treaty that President Monroe wants signed. You are all invited to the giveaway powwow at the Maumee Rapids late next summer."

"Long trip," McCarty explained to the others.

"Also," Perish said, "Could we impose on you for a marriage ceremony?"

McCarty considered Dorothy and Perish who stood closer to each other than was necessary for all practical purposes. "Two young white people want an Indian wedding?"

"Yes." Dorothy stepped forward. "We need one."

"I see." McCarty looked at Ponthe. "Father Tantum is making his missionary rounds. We don't expect him back until the time of singing frogs."

The group of weary treaty ambassadors all shook their heads, no.

"Can't wait that long." McCarty understood.

Supay stepped forward. "I know the words. My mother has had four husbands."

Ponthe laughed, "Didn't seem to take."

"All dead," Supay said.

Ponthe went to the young man. "My apologies. Of course, your words will be perfect for the ceremony."

Supay said, "In the morning, I'm marrying the Commander Clitz's daughter, Charlotte, and Philip Raven. Raven is an army guide from our tribe."

"A double wedding," Perish said.

Dorothy jumped up and down like the child she was.

McCarty interrupted, "Smoke first, then irritating treaty."

"Then wedding fun," Jimmy Sweetwater said.

Perish questioned how he could watch Jimmy's alcohol consumption and get married at the same time.

Then Lieutenant Cass voiced his objections, "Ponthe, Dorothy's mother and the church would not approve."

Ponthe turned, his face changed by a deep frown. "Dorothy," he said, his voice almost a whisper, "I believe Lieutenant Cass is speaking the truth."

Dorothy's stance changed as she accepted the verdict. Her shoulders slumped. He met her glance. Did Dorothy expect him to demand a wedding? Perish put his hand on her back, then nodded. He did understand her disappointment.

* * *

Inside Fort Mackinac's visitors' parlour, Dorothy was pleased to find four white women. A mother could never be substituted, but women understood Dorothy's need for female companionship. The significance of a wedding ceremony, native or white, seemed lost on men. Dorothy already envied for Charlotte Clitz, who was being allowed to marry a native. Someday soon, Dorothy would marry her own Perish. She shook herself. Nothing bad had happened. Lieutenant Cass was right. Mother would not be happy hearing about her wedding. Elizabeth Evans would want to attend her only daughter's marriage. Dorothy tried to imagine how she might be of service to the bride-to-be. St. Frances' prayer included a line about forgetting self in order to find. Her mind presented her with one known fact, brides needed everything to be as perfect as possible.

Major Thomas Howard, a doctor stationed on Drummond Island, had sent his wife to the fort for the winter. After Catherine Howard introduced herself, the next words out of her mouth were, "Major Howard is expected to join us shortly."

"How many days do you have to wait?" Dorothy accepted the china cup filled with tea from the dark-skinned woman, who might have been five years older than Dorothy, making her close to twenty. Dorothy sat down in a straight-backed chair facing a long couch.

"We thought your canoes were his party," Mildred, an older woman said, "I'm Catherine's mother. And the mother of these two." Mildred's white hair was neatly braided into a crown around her temples. She was not as plump as Dorothy's mother.

After adding the sugar and thick cream to her tea, Dorothy reached across the table to touch Catherine's arm. "You're lucky to have your mother with you."

"Is yours dead?" Catherine asked.

Dorothy took in a shocked breath. "No. She's well, I hope. I'll join her in Fort Detroit after we finish the treaty rounds."

A mere whiff of a dark-haired girl, maybe thirteen, struggled to sit still on a silver gray settee next to the window. Suddenly, she stood and danced around the room.

"Mary, Mary, do be still." Mildred scolded the scamp. "Bring the desk chair and sit next to Dorothy. She's my youngest." Then Mildred turned to the slim and stately woman, sitting beside her. "And this is the bride, Charlotte Clots."

Charlotte's hair was as blonde as Perish's.

"I'm so happy to meet you all." Dorothy tried to stop a fresh need to weep. "I didn't realize how much I would miss talking to women."

"Will Dorothy come to Charlotte's wedding?" Mary nearly sang each word.

Catherine and Mildred exchanged glances, while Mary fingered the fringe on the shoulder of Dorothy's dress.

Dorothy worried that the women might find her unacceptable, dressed as a native. She lifted her chin, determined to survive any meanness they might decide to levy. Before Dorothy left Fort Detroit, her mother had warned her some whites were not as loving of natives as she had been taught to be. Dorothy smiled at the gossiping women. They were assessing her as if she were already living in Perish's culture. She hoped to alleviate any need for them to hurt her feelings by her own show of friendliness.

"Where did you trade for this?" Mary chattered on. "Does Fort Detroit have lots of Indians? We do."

"My future mother-in-law made this dress for me," Dorothy said. "My husband-to-be saw me wearing the dress in a vision."

"How romantic." Mildred stood up with her hands busily smoothing her dark skirt. "Does that mean you want to wear buckskin to Charlotte's wedding?"

"It's all I have," Dorothy explained, hoping for help from some direction. Perhaps the abundant universe would provide. She sipped the last of her tea.

Charlotte automatically refilled her cup. "When troops abandoned the fort after the last war, they left a lot of their belongings." Charlotte stood and rocked back on her heels to size up Dorothy's guest potential.

"We assumed the wives wanted us to distribute the clothing among the natives." Mildred stood behind the couch, shaking her head. "They did like the jewelry, but they ripped up the dresses for swaddling clothes for the infants."

"There's a lot left." Mary clapped her hands in anticipation. "Charlotte picked the very best!"

"Would you like to choose something to wear to the wedding?" Charlotte replaced her tea cup on the tea serving tray.

"There's an unusual number of fancy dresses." Catherine stood and motioned for Dorothy to accompany her. The rest of the ladies followed them up the servant stairs to the second floor of the officers' lodging.

"Mary," Mildred directed. "Run down and ask Antonette to have more tea sent up."

Up another flight of stairs in a third floor attic room, dresses were hung on clothes lines under dust covers of sheets and blankets. After the women pulled back the coverings, Dorothy saw more finery in one room than she had ever seen. A dressing table sat under one gabled window. A pedestal mirror awaited her transformation. She chose the simplest light blue gown. Hand-sown pearls graced the skirt as well as the high neck of the shimmering silk dress.

"My skin is so dark," Dorothy said as she reached out to touch the dress.

"At first," Mary squealed, "We thought you were a native."

Charlotte hushed her. "Perish North is a beautiful young man."

"He's half-native." Dorothy wanted to keep the record straight. "But his hair is every much as blond as yours, Charlotte."

"And handsome," Catherine smiled at her.

"Yes," Dorothy said. "A kinder, more honorable man can't be found."

"You are in love." Mildred pushed a strand of hair behind Dorothy's ear. "And you are a ravishing beauty."

Dorothy's heart tugged at the memory of her mother's action in the Fort Detroit garden, when she had introduced Beauty. After donning the beautiful dress, Dorothy turned to look in the mirror, surprised at the image before her. "Perish might not recognize me."

Supay's wife, Antonette, brought a tea tray into the women's sanctum. "Father Tantum took his Bible with him."

"Lieutenant Cass has one," Dorothy didn't mention the Bible's previous owner.

"The Ottawa marriage ceremony words are just like poetry," Catherine said. "I married Thomas with them."

Dorothy reconsidered for a moment. She wondered if Thomas or even Catherine might be part native. But, her mother would want more than a native ceremony to celebrate her marriage to Perish. "There are a few verses about a man cleaving to his wife in the Bible."

"We don't have many flowers for the church." Charlotte worried her brows.

"Would Perish North wear a suit?" Antonette asked. "Just for the ceremony. Raven, I mean Philip Raven, will be dressed."

"Perhaps Supay could ask?" Dorothy held out the long skirt of her dress. "I wouldn't mind either way. Could Supay suggest appropriate apparel to Ponthe Walker, too?"

"Perish is from a noble Huron family." Antonette bowed as if to leave.

"I miss my mother." Dorothy was still transfixed by the beauty in the mirror -- herself.

"Give me her address," Mildred said. "I'll write to her. I know all the details she will want to hear about Charlotte's wedding, and your transformation."

"Everything." Catherine laughed. "We could use the rest of the veils to decorate the altar.

"Oh yes," Mary jumped up and down with excitement. "I'll decorate the bridal suite, too. I'm going to be Charlotte's maid of honor." Mary made little hops around the room.

"Do you think she can stand still long enough?" Charlotte laughed.

* * *

Perish asked Lieutenant Cass, if they should dress for the next morning's wedding ceremony. Lieutenant Cass said. "We could. Apparently there are clothes in the attic of the officer quarters."

Across the hall from the attic room, where the dresses kept Dorothy enthralled, another storage room contained discarded male clothing. Dust covered everything. Ponthe opened a beat-up trunk and the lid fell backwards off the rusty hinges. A cloud of dirt and lint rose from the floor. The stale air assaulted their lungs. Perish struggled to open a window that had been painted shut. "This is worst than trapping."

Ponthe broke the window with his elbow. "You liked our hunting trips."

"At least I could breathe outside."

"We have to stay in here until you find something to wear." Lieutenant Cass' tone indicated the task hopeless. He held up a pair of pants that both he and Perish could have stood in, a man for each leg. "Dorothy is across the hall, choosing a dress to attend the Commander's daughter's wedding." Lieutenant Cass delved into another trunk, then held up two white shirts. He measured one sleeve by holding it to his shoulder. "Bull's-eye."

"I can wear the other," Perish said. "Ponthe, are you planning to dress too?"

"No," he said. "I'll stay who I am."

Perish sat down hard on another trunk. "I don't even know who I am. Native or white?"

"You're both," Lieutenant Cass said. "The Lord needs bridges between peoples."

Shaking his head as Lieutenant Cass looked around for another trunk to open, Ponthe said, "I'd stay with the trunk where you found the shirts."

"Shoes!" Perish dumped over a trunk. "The shoelaces are tied together."

Lieutenant Cass nodded. "Women do that so the pairs don't get lost."

"Bet you won't find any socks." Ponthe rested against an exposed roof joist.

"We could use your help, Sir." Perish thought Lieutenant Cass was going to salute his father.

Ponthe laughed. "Coup counted." Ponthe started rummaging through the trunks.

"Mercy," Lieutenant Cass said, clearly impressed.

Perish wondered if Lieutenant Cass understood the importance of, 'coup-counted.' Instead of killing an enemy, braves would settle for touching the chest of an opponent, counting the deed as more important than a death. Ponthe had graciously allowed the lieutenant to order him around.

Three trunks held folded handkerchiefs, socks, suspenders, and long johns. Perish withdrew to the farthest corner. He turned and took off his breechcloth. Balancing carefully on one foot he stepped into a pair of pants with legs that seemed the right length. The wool scratched his skin. "Throw me a pair of those long johns," he hollered.

Lieutenant Cass tossed him one pair after another. Ponthe joined in raining long underwear on Perish.

"Enough, enough." Perish finally laughed. "Father, I'm not sure I want to join the white race."

"You do," Ponthe said. "Temporarily."

"At least for the church wedding," Lieutenant Cass said. "You can toss the clothes back up here as soon as you finished with them."

Perish wondered if he would be expected to dress in these black clothes in the future, if Dorothy wanted to live in town, after they married. He didn't like the clothes. He loved Dorothy. Maybe she loved him enough as he was, dressed as a native.

"Things fall together, son." Ponthe seemed to read Perish/s mind. He presented Perish with a pile of black dress jackets over his arm. "Dorothy will let you know what she wants and when she wants it."

Perish tried on several hats, discarding them all. "What if she thinks I'll stay in these clothes?"

Ponthe moved Perish's long braids behind his ears and tied them together. "What indeed?"

* * *

The chapel of Fort Mackinac's church was just large enough to hold all the inhabitants of the fort. Indian families in their beaded finery vied with soldiers for the best seats. Before the ceremony, an officer, Samuel Finnemore, played "Greensleeves" on a brass flute.

Dorothy felt like dancing with the native footsteps Antonette had taught her for the Ottawa ceremony to follow. Major Thomas Howard's joyful arrival hadn't deterred Catherine, Mildred or Mary from performing a miracle on the church. Instead of poky pews, lace-trimmed, net clouds lined the aisles. In front of the altar, a billowing veiled arbor held Philip Raven in drab, civilized clothes. His copper gorget was his only native ornament.

When Dorothy first viewed suited Perish with his blond braids pulled behind his ears, her heart reached for the handsome man she loved.

Perish smiled and offered his arm. "Dorothy, you're lovelier than the bride."

But Dorothy missed all the familiar angles and slopes of Perish's body. The muscles on his shoulders and arms were hidden by black cloth. Even his trim waist was concealed by his jacket. She wondered if she seemed as un-feminine to him as he seemed less male in his new attire. His eyes appeared entranced with her beaded blue dress. Perish's nostrils flared and he was smiling. The lilac perfume she chose from Catherine's collection performed the scent's promise.

Supay's words, both native and biblical, were lost in Dorothy's haze of borrowed happiness. After Perish had touched her hand as the couple kissed, Dorothy knew he was under all that black cloth, somewhere, thinking about their future ceremony.

Snow began falling as soon as the newly married couple, Mr. and Mrs. Philip Raven, stepped outside the church. Dorothy had to laugh when Perish stuck out his tongue to taste the petals of ice. She held out her hand to the snow's freshness and her palm was quickly covered in huge melting stars.

After Dorothy and Perish changed back into their traveling buckskins, the Ottawa ceremonies were danced through inches of fresh snow. Charlotte wore a white deerskin robe trimmed in white fur.

The rhythmic drumbeats and native calls produced more physical reactions than the cold visual stimuli and churched words. Though she wanted the promises of forever spoken, Dorothy hadn't really paid attention to the vows. This stomping and swaying in the soft snow seemed more in keeping with her body's awareness of Perish.

* * *

Amidst the falling snow, wearing Beauty's dress, Dorothy danced in the women's circle surrounding the inner circle of men. Her long raven hair, freed of its braiding, was dusted with snow. Perish judged his future wife the best dancer. She was the only one who interested him. When her eyes met his in passing, they held all the welcome he reciprocated. He wanted the dance to continue forever, like the promises Charlotte and Philip made when Perish had worn the moldy-smelling clothes. On the other hand, Perish fought a strong impulse to grasp his slim girl and run to a private place, away from the assembled guests.

Supay handed a reed to Philip Raven. Charlotte Raven was directed to hold the other end of the rod and dance with him. Witnesses to the ceremony broke off pieces of the rod until the couple's hands touched with the promise of being united as one, forever.

Perish moved closer to Dorothy as the dance ended. He kissed her eager lips. "We'll soon be together."

She kissed him in return. "I'm so tired," she said, before falling sound asleep on his shoulder.

Perish carried her into the women's quarters. He laid her on one of the dormitory's bed and left before anyone could scold him.

When morning hadn't yet lightened the sky, Dorothy crept out of the bed with a blanket about her. The fire in the cold large room's fireplace had gone out. She restarted a fire in the grate before climbing back into bed. How could her mother live so long without a husband? Dorothy decided she would never live alone, no matter how old she got. Surely, Perish would remain within reach.

December it was, the days were still getting shorter. She hoped they could stay at the fort for Christmas celebrations. When she had kissed Perish, she was borne away on her emotions. As she lay on her back, she was content to dream of their future together on the trip. They still owned every day of the rest of our lives. "Please, Lord," Dorothy prayed for their future.

* * *

Breakfast with Perish in the crowded mess hall was not romantic.

Ponthe announced they would be leaving. "The snow won't stop falling until it reaches four or five feet."

"How does he know?" Dorothy asked Perish, disappointed about missing Christmas.

Ponthe answered for him. "There is no wind. That means the storm is not moving off, and it can snow until next spring."

"We have to leave," Lieutenant Cass said, "or Lake Michigan will freeze before we reach Wisconsin."

Dorothy shivered. Catherine was sitting across the long table from her. "Do you have woolen under things?"

"Cotton," Dorothy answered.

"Come with me," Mildred said.

In their sleeping quarters, the women showed Dorothy how to pull the scratchy woolen long johns over her cotton drawers and stockings. Dorothy hadn't realized the full extent of living outdoors in winter. The campfires never thoroughly warmed her and the canoes were without heat of any kind. Her fur-lined coat did provide some relief. The men seemed more accustomed to being outside in the winter.

"You'll need this too." Antonette produced a soft knit cap that could be pulled down over her chin. Eye sockets mouth, and hair openings were provided.

Catherine kissed her good-bye. "Wear it as a neck scarf, until you need to pull it up."

"At least my ears won't fall off from the cold," Dorothy said. "I don't know how to thank you."

"Could we keep the Bible you loaned us for the wedding?" Charlotte asked. "The winter is so long up here."

"Of course," Dorothy said.

In the dormitory, Dorothy rummaged through her satchel with her back to the other women. Finding the heavy Bible that Lieutenant Cass had lent Charlotte, she tore out the first few pages with Bishop Pascal's notations of family records. She stuffed them into the bottom of the bag. 'Surely the Lord will forgive me,' she prayed. I'm protecting Dasquorant from being accused wrongly, in case anyone notices the Bishop is not with us. But, now I'll have nothing to read. As she handed over the Bible to Charlotte, she saw Perish standing at the door. Had he shared her concerns?

"Lieutenant Cass was given four books from the officers." Perish shouldered both their packs of supplies. "Perhaps he'll let you read them."

Dorothy smiled up at the man who did belong only to her. "Marriage will never turn me into a weakling." She reclaimed her backpack.

Chapter Eight

Lake Michigan

The canoes slid easily from the snow-covered rocks of the shore into the cold lake. The men put their socks and boots on after they got in the boats.

"Terrible way to wake up," Henry complained.

Lieutenant Cass waved to four soldiers on the shore. One of them made the sign of the cross in a farewell blessing.

Dorothy's canoe with Perish at the helm came alongside the bigger canoe. "Lieutenant Cass," Dorothy called. "Perish tells me you have four new books with you."

"I do," he said, manning his paddle. "You're welcome to borrow them."

"I left the Bible with Charlotte," Dorothy explained, "in return for warmer clothing." She reached for Lieutenant Cass's paddle, not making the mistake of leaning over too far. "What did you trade for the books?"

"Not your coffee beans." He laughed. "I'm carrying letters for their families. I'll post them when I get to Fort Meigs."

"I wish I had paper to write Mother," Dorothy said.

Perish turned to her. "I can strip birch off a tree as soon as we land. You could keep a journal for her. When you go to the Washington school, I'll take it to her."

"No!" Dorothy shouted. She sobered after her outburst. "I'm staying with you." She would miss the opportunity to be educated, formally. But being with Perish had always been her goal. The Bishop had convinced Dorothy's mother she needed the nuns at the Washington convent to properly train her mind to think in rigorous patterns. But now she knew Bishop Pascal's unholy reasons for wanting her on the treaty trip. Please forgive him, Lord. And me, Dorothy added. After all, she had not been entirely truthful in agreeing to go to the Washington school when the trip was completed. All along she had known her reasons for becoming the camp's cook was to be as close as possible to Perish. She needed to prove she could thrive as a native's wife, to him. She could always pick up a book, when her curiosity demanded answers.

Perish had stopped paddling.

Ponthe caught up with them. "What's the problem, children?" Neither of the grown-up children replied. Ponthe smiled. "Oh, family business."

"No! Wait!" Dorothy called. "Perish thinks I'm still going to school in Washington."

"Aren't you?" Ponthe asked.

"Of course not, we're supposed to stay together. We're going to marry."

Crane called from the rear of the big canoe. "Anything wrong?"

"We'll catch up." Ponthe called back.

* * *

Perish turned in the boat to face his father and Dorothy. What had he done wrong now?

Ponthe had moved his canoe close to Dorothy's end of their canoe. He put his arm around her. "What makes you think Perish won't stay with you in Washington?"

"He said he would take my journal to my mother in Fort Detroit. All my plans to marry Perish are slipping past me faster than Lake Michigan is passing the canoes."

"I can take the journal," Ponthe said.

"He wants to live apart from me." Dorothy started to cry. "Like you and Beauty."

"Do you, son?"

"No," Perish finally said. Dorothy's moods changed faster than the weather. He was entering an unknown forest, unsure of his footing. Maybe women were basically the same. Maybe that's why Ponthe found it difficult to stay around his mother. But he knew enough to walk softly, to not disturb a twig or leaf lest a frightened animal attack him. He would breathe softly and watch. She was such a lovely thing, even now. Her face was red, her nose dripping, her eyes squinting to keep unshed tears at bay. "I love being with her." He meant his words.

Dorothy didn't seem convinced. She looked at Ponthe for some reassurance.

"Now, Dorothy," Ponthe said. "We love you, but you're going to have to paddle like your life depended on it, so we can catch up to

Crane. It's too hard to keep up, when we're not in the big boat's lee. We might capsize in these rough waters."

* * *

No more needed to be said. Dorothy had already experienced being dumped in a river. And according to Henry's horror stories, this Lake Michigan had no bottom. She paddled with all her might, stroke after stroke, for hours and hours. Her arms felt like they could fall off, her shoulders burned from the exertion. But, her heart had stopped hurting and her tears were dry.

She wanted to see Perish's face. Was he angry with her? But Perish couldn't turn around and paddle at the same time. So she sent her words to him, trying to lace them with a loving tone. "Nature is so beautiful it fills my soul. Have you seen all the Great Lakes?"

Perish nodded. "Lake Superior is a wonder when it is calm. The vastness and quiet solitude do soothe the mind. You can count pebbles in the waterbed at 20 feet."

"Erie means long tail, right?" Dorothy relaxed. Her future husband was not upset that she made a row about Washington. The strength of his movements while he propelled their canoe threw the frigid lake reassured her of his protection. His manliness awed her at times. Was he even growing taller? Maybe only in the size he commanded in her heart.

"Huron is the French word for Wyandot." Perish recited the names. "Michigan is Chippewa for great water, 'michigami.' Ontario is a Huron word for great lake."

"I haven't seen the northern lights. Have you?" Dorothy asked. Perish's knowledge of the great outdoors seemed to diminish the warehouse of facts her brain could recite from the books in Father Sebastian's library.

"No, but I've read about them," Perish said. "They say you never get over the experience. The sheer force of nature shown in the rocks along the lakeshores amazes me, too."

"The Bible says mountains skipped like young deer," Dorothy said. "I guess that's when an earthquake happens."

"Volcanoes must be frightening, too." Perish shuddered.

"I think they're the reason people believe in hell, do you?"

Perish shook his head. "Life is so hard for people. This is all we need of punishment. I think the Christians have something in the promise of forgiveness if we forgive others."

- 81 -

"You and I have had easy lives, if you want to compare us to other settlers, or tribes. I think you right about the people who call themselves Christian, but the Savior doesn't only forgive. I think they believe he provides everything, if they ask."

A gigantic cloud of pigeons swept overhead, covering half the sky, nearly dimming the sun.

"There's glory for you," Dorothy said.

"We are close to our creator," Perish agreed. "The Great Spirit of all."

* * *

The campsite that evening on the northern-most coast of Lake Michigan afforded the travelers protection from a wicked west wind. The snow had stopped as the wind rose. A cleft in the rocky cliffs sheltered a space large enough for a generous fire. A cave-like formation provided further freedom from the cold. Burnt wood near a hollowed-out space in the sand at the cave's entrance showed this site was a favorite for lake travelers.

Crane and Flat Belly had trailed nets in the water. The smell of fish in the frying pan, coffee, and roasted potatoes from the fort heightened the appetites of the tired voyagers.

Inside the cave area, Perish set up Dorothy's tent. Maybe Dorothy was getting too tired to talk. He wanted to prove to her that he would stay with her, no matter what she decided about school.

After the camp supper, Perish wondered why Dorothy carried a kettle full of hot water into the tent. It took Perish a minute to realize she was planning to bathe. As soon as she sat the pot down inside the tent, Perish kissed the back of her neck, where the braids parted. "Forgive me about mentioning Washington?"

"In order to love someone you have to be able to forgive." Dorothy turned toward him.

Perish wished she was more cheerful about it. "I don't want you to feel it's your duty."

"Duty?" Dorothy asked.

"I mean." He'd messed up again. "If you're too tired to talk about Washington, I understand."

"Are you too tired?"

"No," he said. Still he wanted to be sure Dorothy's mood was conducive to the topic of her educational needs. He tried to introduce a safe subject to test her reaction. "I wish I hadn't been so eager to get rid of my woolens. White people know how to keep warm."

"You didn't freeze last winter."

It would have helped if Dorothy had agreed with him about something. Arguing left him feeling separated from her. Perish left her tent and made a bedroll at the entrance. Maybe he was more tired than he thought. Attempting to talk about Washington seemed a chore. His heart wasn't in it. He wished he knew how to fake a convincing snore.

* * *

Dorothy ached all over. All she needed was a touch from Perish to ease all her pains away. But no, he had to get into some philosophical discussion about the merits of white civilization. She worried Perish might think she'd been too cantankerous. He loved her. "I'm never going to stop loving you," she promised him in her heart.

Crane and Lieutenant Cass had kept the fire roaring at the mouth of the cave throughout the night. The smell of bacon woke Dorothy. She had failed her job as cook. She scrambled into her deerskin dress. "I'll start the biscuits and coffee," she told Perish as she stepped over him.

As Dorothy set the pot to boil with porridge, her eyes challenged Ponthe to say even one word of censure about her lateness.

"I thought I would hear all sorts of interesting noises from you two." Henry Holt was irrepressible as usual.

"Jeez," Jimmy Sweetwater said. "You can't talk about that."

"But there wasn't a hint of ruckus," Henry insisted. "Are you two still mad at each other?"

Dorothy's blush matched Perish's. "Young man you will remember your manners or you will not eat."

Henry appealed to Ponthe. "What?"

Dorothy was up to this task. She cupped Henry's chin in her hand and placed her fingertip on the ridge between his nose and upper lip. "The Lord gave you this ridge when the angels brought you into the world." She smacked him on the top of the head. "You're supposed to keep silent about how babies are made."

"Oh," the youngster said. "Do you have to get married because you're pregnant?"

Perish rose belligerently, intending to do harm.

"Silence," Ponthe commanded. "Henry, you are saying that my son and his wife-to-be are not honorable people." He towered over Henry. "Is that what you intended?"

"No, Sir." Henry said. "I did not, and I'm sorry if that's what my curiosity sounded like." He brushed his forehead of hair. "Can I eat now, please?"

Dorothy took pity on him and handed him a bowl with two pieces of bacon on top. "Thanks," he said.

She could see a hint of tears in his eyes. Henry turned away and concentrated on his food. "Bit harsh," she whispered to Ponthe, as she handed him his food.

"I don't think so," Ponthe whispered back.

* * *

The next day's work seemed easier to Perish. Dorothy chatted almost all day. Perish was glad of it. Her silences were harder to understand. Ponthe said they would have to wait until sundown to stop, or Sturgeon Bay wouldn't be reached before ice trapped them on the lake. That morning they had pushed the canoes for almost an hour on the frozen lake before ominous cracking cued them into jumping into the crafts before their feet got wet.

"Why are the Ottawa richer than the Seneca?" Dorothy continued her discourse.

"The Ottawa do trade more with other tribes." Perish loved the way Dorothy's voice eased his shoulders into the stride of paddling. He knew as a help-mate for life, Dorothy would make every day brighter, more meaningful. Although he was not accustomed to constantly carrying on a continuing conversation, he said, "The Seneca have always relied on the land to yield wealth."

"Like the English and us."

"Us?" Perish asked.

"Americans."

Perish hoped his back didn't reveal his quandary. Did Dorothy realize he wasn't sure if he was an American, Potawatomi, or Huron? "Do you and your mother own land?"

He thought that was a safe question. He had to watch what he said to his future wife, especially because she might think he was as white as his hair. Which he wasn't, as far as he knew...in his heart.

"No," Dorothy said. "We're not rich enough. Does Beauty own her camp on the Raisin River?"

"The land is covered in the treaty we're carrying." Perish knew what the underlying question was. "Where should we settle?"

"Is there room for us at your mother's?"

Perish turned around to give Dorothy his best smile. "She'd love to have us close."

Dorothy remained silent for a long time, too long.

Perish's hopes for immediate peace between them vanished. Was married life going to be even more difficult? Maybe they were not destined to be together. He tried to recall his vision at Copper Harbor. As swift as the wind, his memory of the red-spotted dress and the lovely muse wearing it appeared before him. Dorothy was to be his wife, to mother generations of his children. "We could find a place to live in Washington," Perish said, hoping to stave off trouble.

"Which do you want?"

He didn't really know. "All I know is that I want you to be happy with me."

"Good answer." Ponthe's canoe had sidled up to theirs. "I'm going ahead to hunt for meat. We're going to need all the energy we can get."

Dorothy hadn't answered Perish yet. He didn't want to bring up the subject again. Maybe things would work out naturally.

"We'll agree on whatever we decide," Dorothy said quietly.

Perish turned to her, overcome with relief. "We will."

* * *

It was strange, Dorothy often felt older than Perish. He was three years her senior. Nevertheless, he didn't have a clue about how he wanted to live his life when they married. Would they be happy living with Beauty on the Raisin River? Dorothy tried to imagine a life without furniture, without books, without curtains, without.... She wouldn't think about it. Eight months was a long time to think about the future.

If she became pregnant after they married, the Dominican nuns in Washington wouldn't accept her as a student anyway. Oh, they might let her leave the child with them. She was sure of one thing. No nun would raise any child of hers while she yet lived. But the convent wouldn't let her study as a married woman with the other girls. She might corrupt them with her knowledge of good and evil.

Poor Henry. No one seemed to understand. He wanted to know as soon as possible what all the fuss about sex was. That's all. He wasn't ornery. He was an innocent. Why shouldn't he know all the facts as soon as possible? Ponthe should take him aside. Questions needed to be answered, or curiosity could get twisted into unhealthy pursuits.

She called after Ponthe as his canoe moved past them. "Take Henry with you, and tell him what he needs to know."

"Good idea," Ponthe said. "Smart girl," he said to Perish as he passed.

"Too smart?" Dorothy asked Perish after Ponthe was out of earshot.

Perish shook his head. "I need all the help I can get from my partner."

Dorothy laughed and mimicked Ponthe's voice, "Good answer."

* * *

Sturgeon Bay

Sturgeon Bay was the coldest place Dorothy had ever been. The wind whipped around them from both the lake and the bay. Captain Pipe's Delaware village of stone wigwams provided some shelter. The surface of the stones inside the meetinghouse were frosted knee-high from the natives' warmth. A dozen or so natives arranged themselves around an open firepit in the center of the room, as the treaty travelers entered. An aperture in the rounded ceiling dispersed the smoke.

Mounted opposite the east entrance, the Red Score history of the grandfather tribe of the Iroquois was carved on broad wooden paddles. The travelers bowed before each carving. Perish briefly told her the history of the three major divisions: the wolf, turtle, and turkey. They had served in Pontiac's rebellion, Little Turtle's War, and finally Tecumseh's fight.

After the hosts and travelers shared an abundant dinner of fresh moose meat, Ponthe was asked to present the sparse treaty allocations. He stood facing the entrance of the meeting room. "Article 19 provides nine square miles on the Sandusky River for the Delaware. Zeechawon, named James Armstrong, will head the tribe. The four chiefs invited to the treaty powwow on the Maumee will each receive 640 acres: Kithtuwheland or Anderson, Puchbrich or

Captain Beaver, Tahunquecoppi or your old chief Captain Pipe, and Aweabiesa or Whirlwind"

No one spoke.

Captain Pipe, a frail old man, rose from his seated position and went to the red-painted paddles. He touched each one reverently, then returned to his seat among the three other chiefs. The old man called Anderson appeared to be a half-breed. Captain Beaver and Whirlwind were younger members of the tribe.

Armstrong stood next to Ponthe when he spoke. "Captain Pipe has honored our ancestors with this knowledge. The time of peace is welcomed. Babies need to be born, couples need to worry less."

Captain Beaver and Whirlwind nodded assent to each other.

Dorothy caught Henry's look. He winked. Apparently, Ponthe had done a thorough job of educating the boy.

Armstrong wore buckskin devoid of ornament except for his long black bear cape. "Our fallen comrades will watch over us. They will help us prevail against the evil ways of the white race."

Evil ways? Dorothy's thoughts had briefly turned to her future with Perish. Her pleasant plans about being able to explore his person, once they were married, were snagged by Armstrong's words. White people, including herself, were thieves of the land. When she asked Perish where they would live, Dorothy really meant what parcel of native land could they claim for themselves. She started to weep at the injustices, at her own avariciousness. Much to her embarrassment, she couldn't stop loud sobs.

Ponthe motioned for Perish to take her outside.

"It's freezing," Perish said instead.

Dorothy sobbed on.

"She's sorry for our brethren." Perish touched his own yellow hair. "Our sins against the true owners of the land will never be erased."

Ponthe bowed to him, indicating Perish should continue.

"Each calamity: each day it rains when white men need sun; each day of drought, each day of numbing frost, each fevered brain can be laid at the feet of whites, who can't understand the land belongs to all people, instead of those with fences."

The Delaware murmured their agreement, nodding to each other.

Then a pain started deep in Dorothy's stomach, reaching her throat. She let out a loud scream. Another followed as her stomach jumped inside her. Then she felt the warm blood. She looked at Ponthe for help, instead of Perish.

"Is there a place?" Ponthe asked Armstrong.

Armstrong nodded, wrapped his fur around his shoulders, and headed for the door.

Ponthe took off his own winter wrap and covered Dorothy before picking her up. "Relax, little one," he said. "Nature is having its way."

Dorothy fainted with the next onslaught of pain.

* * *

Perish sat with Dorothy throughout the night. Ponthe had patiently explained how Dorothy's monthly cycle, after a lapse of time, and the cold, were causing her such discomfort.

And my curse on white men. Perish had condemned himself, his future wife, and maybe their children...as white people. Forgive me, Orenda, Great Spirit...

Dorothy moaned in her sleep. The prophet, Delaware, had forbidden alcohol, but the natives had other potent painkillers, which they had graciously shared.

She had heard his words of denunciation. Would she ever forgive him?

* * *

Dorothy awoke without pain. Perish was holding her hand. She squeezed it, and his eyes popped open.

"Are you in pain?"

"No. What happened to me?"

"Ponthe told me it was probably your monthly cycle kicking in after a long delay." He kissed her cheek tenderly.

She wrapped her arm around his neck. "I'm glad I'm a woman again. I'm hungry."

Dorothy started to get out of the bedroll but Perish pushed her down. "I'll bring you some porridge." He arranged her backpack behind her, so she was almost in a sitting position.

"Thanks," she said. "Coffee and a full kettle of hot water."

She waited until the porridge and coffee hit her stomach, just to make sure no pain was going to sweep away her senses. "When do we leave?"

"Ponthe says you will need a week."

"For what?"

"Native women are separated from others during their monthly cycles. They don't cook our food, or touch us."

"Get Ponthe."

"No," Perish said slowly as if teaching a child manners. "Ponthe said I should explain our ways to you."

* * *

"Get out, Perish." At least he knew enough to do what he was told. "Tell Ponthe I'll talk to the men," Dorothy called after him.

Dorothy cleaned herself up and dressed quickly. Outside, the voyagers stood around in a scattered group. Dorothy asked, "Ponthe, will the Delaware allow us to speak together, without them in the main lodge?"

As the Delaware men left the biggest stone lodge, Ponthe signaled for Dorothy and the others to enter.

Inside the warm room, Dorothy motioned for the men to sit down. "Ponthe, you know Whipping Stick only talked to her husband when she wanted the tribe to know her mind, but Perish has too many elders in our camp for my words to carry any power."

Perish and the other men nodded to each other. Ponthe didn't take his attention away from her.

Dorothy continued her argument. "Crane and Flat Belly, you know my mother cooked for the priest every day of every month. No one died."

Then she faced Ponthe again. "White women are not content to sit for a week while their bodies accommodate the rules of men. I am able and willing to continue the trip today. If any of you find my presence distasteful, you can either starve or fix your own food."

Ponthe bowed his head. "Little Daughter, if you say you are ready to travel, I can only submit to your wishes. None in the camp will stay away from your meals. Our Delaware brothers will be surprised that we continue the trip so soon."

"Perish," Dorothy asked with some deference, "May I return to my tent to pack now?"

Perish nodded, and led the way out of the meeting building.

The Delaware stood with their faces to the building. They didn't turn around when Perish and Dorothy exited.

* * *

Inside the large, stone guest-wigwam, where Perish had hung Dorothy's tent for her privacy, Dorothy set to work gathering their belongings.

"I'm proud of you," Perish managed. "...for standing up to my father."

Dorothy sat down on her backpack. Perish thought she must have felt more pain and rushed to her, kneeling at her side.

"Quit fussing," Dorothy said, pushing him backward.

Perish's balance hadn't been good and he fell over. She laughed at him then covered her mouth. Still smiling she said, "That was our first clash of cultures."

Perish nodded. "And we're both white."

"Sometimes," she hung her head, suddenly shy.

"What is it?"

"Is there a native ceremony for women when they return from the isolation time?"

"Not that I know of." Perish was happy to be ignorant of the matter. "Beauty and I lived somewhat separate from the other Potawatomi, even though they loved us. I can't wait until we're married. I mean, I'll be a happy man."

Her smile returned and she picked up her load without a hitch.

* * *

Outside, Ponthe approached them from a gathering of the Delaware around their canoes. She wondered why Flat Belly and Crane were loading supplies onto Henry and Jimmy's backpacks. Lieutenant Cass' pack reached high above his head.

"We'll make better time if we trade our canoes for snowshoes now." Ponthe handed Perish two pairs.

"We can't trade snowshoes for canoes once we reach the Illinois." Lieutenant Cass seemed worried.

Ponthe held out a purse of coins. "We can purchase canoes with this money."

Lieutenant Cass passed it to Dorothy who stood between the officer and Perish. Before giving the purse to Perish, Dorothy pulled out one coin. It had a square hole in it.

Ponthe answered her question. "Chinese. Some of the Delaware returned from the plains, unhappy with the way they were treated by the other tribes."

"Did they speak of Dasquorant?" Perish asked.

"I inquired," Ponthe closed the subject.

"How many camps before we reach the Illinois River?" Dorothy asked running the list of supplies through her head.

"With snowshoes only a week."

"Is there a supply fort for provisions?" she asked.

Jimmy Sweetwater seemed happy to report, "Fort Dearborn."

"We need to meet the Potawatomi there," Ponthe said.

"Is that still a week away?" Dorothy asked.

"Four days if we can get started." Ponthe laughed.

Dorothy didn't move. As Ponthe turned his back to start the trek, Dorothy called after him, "Ponthe, we will need meat at least three of the four days."

Ponthe turned around and nearly bowed. "May I send Perish, Clan Mother?" he winked at her.

She agreed and they were off. Dorothy was amazed at her own body's ability to adapt to the strenuous life she was leading. It was not an effort to keep up with the men, even though she had only played around with snowshoes at Fort Detroit. The long hikes and canoe work had given her muscles a strength she never imagined. White women were not pampered on the Old Northwest frontier, but they rarely had to endure the challenges her young body was meeting and enjoying.

Perish still found it necessary to hover, before he set out to hunt. "You are okay?"

"Never better," she said. "Better hurry, or Ponthe will blame me."

Positioning one of his snowshoe between hers, he took his time kissing her good-bye for the day. "I have chosen the best wife a man could ask for," he whispered.

The sin of pride rose up in Dorothy's heart.

* * *

Part of the trip to Fort Dearborn was spent snowshoeing on the Fox River. The frozen river lay between high banks on both sides. The sunken riverbed gave the line of travelers a buffer from the steady west winds off the plains.

Ponthe led the way with Henry and Jimmy struggling to stay in his tracks. Flat Belly, and Lieutenant Cass followed with Dorothy behind them. Crane brought up the rear.

The trip had created a family of them. Perish, Flat Belly, and Crane were the best hunters. Lieutenant Cass and Ponthe found the best camping sites, and Henry and Jimmy shared firewood and water-carrying duties. Ponthe was truly the father figure Dorothy had never known. Flat Belly and Crane acted like Perish's favorite uncles. And, Henry and Jimmy felt like little brothers, or cousins, to Dorothy.

Dorothy liked cooking for her appreciative audience. Every cup of coffee, every biscuit was taken with thanks. She no longer experienced the chore as unending or meaningless. Instead, pride was growing for her skills at the campfire.

She took pleasure in her ability to comfort, too. Perish's black moods seemed to occur less often. He was happy living as a native. She was too, temporarily.

Chapter Nine

Fort Dearborn

It was unusual to travel so late in the day. Ponthe could have misjudged their closeness to Fort Dearborn. Ponthe had encouraged Dorothy to use up the rest of the food supplies at their noon campsite. Unless they reached the fort soon, no supper or breakfast would be available. Not even coffee could be offered.

The sky held a modicum of slate blue light and the trail was getting darker. Finally, the lights of the fort winked through the trees. Perish joined the synchronized sigh of relief of the travelers. His father was getting older. This trip was taking its toll on Ponthe. Instead of getting stronger like Dorothy, Ponthe seemed to move slower. A third of the trip was still ahead of them.

Perish moved closer to the front of the line. "Let me take your pack, Father. You can greet the Commander more easily."

Perish was surprised Ponthe gladly gave over his burden. "Thank you, Hehawalk. It has been a long trail."

Perish vowed to keep his obsession with Dorothy under better control. His father needed his strength and attention as much as she did, maybe more. Dorothy mentioned at Fort Mackinac she would want a Bible verse included in their vows. The verse had something to do with leaving his father and mother and clinging only unto each other. No. The word was 'cleaving.' At the time, he'd liked the sound of the intimate-sounding word. Nevertheless, his adopted native parents might need his somewhat divided attention for many years to come. He hoped.

Inside Fort Dearborn, cries arose from the crowds on all sides, welcoming the famous Ponthe Walker. Ponthe straightened at the cheers. Perish couldn't help but suspect the cause. He had recognized his mother's work. Sure enough, Ed Renault and Beauty emerged from the crowd.

Renault picked Ponthe up, snowshoes and all, then set him down.

Ponthe regained his dignity before Beauty embraced him. "Husband, you have been gone from my side too long."

Perish helped Dorothy take off her snowshoes as Beauty knelt to untie Ponthe's.

"I can do that." Dorothy pulled him up.

"Father is too tired," Perish whispered close to her ear.

Dorothy's head went up like a frightened deer. "Is he ill?"

Perish continued to whisper. "I'm afraid I haven't been making allowances for his age."

Gigantic Renault swept them up in a dual embrace. "Crane tells me you will marry soon."

Beauty had joined them. "Well that was the plan." She hugged Dorothy, then took Perish's hand.

Perish was disappointed, so he wrapped his arms around his mother, pulled her to his chest. "Mother."

Perish wanted to say he missed her. Was she okay? Why was she here? Did she notice Ponthe had aged from the trip? Could he please just go home! But he was a man now. All those feelings had to be stilled, accepted as his burden. They did weigh on his soul.

Conscious of Dorothy's feelings, he said instead, "Dorothy would make her mother proud." Then he asked, "Is Ponthe going to be all right for the rest of the trip?"

Beauty nodded, but didn't relinquish his hand. "You, my strong son, are doing very well too."

Perish felt like weeping. She understood his feelings without words. "Why are you and Renault so far from the Raisin River?"

"In winter?" Dorothy added. "Is my mother safe and well?"

"She is," Beauty said. "I'm sure. You'll have to forgive me, Dorothy. I didn't visit Fort Detroit before we set out. I had a dream."

Perish noticed when Beauty let go of his hand. He genuinely felt more alone, left to manage his manhood on his own. He coughed to hide his emotion.

Ponthe and Renault had come closer to the threesome.

"Did you tell them your dream?" Renault asked.

Ponthe shook his head. "Another dream."

* * *

Renault pushed Ponthe into the mess hall, where the rest of the travelers were already eating. They gathered at a long table away from the others.

"I dreamt my son was injured." Beauty sat down hard on the bench. Perish knew by her lifted chin and straight spine she was hurt by Ponthe's disbelief and sarcastic tone.

Perish turned his attention to his father, who waved his hand toward his son as if to dismiss the worry.

"You can see he's unmarked." Ponthe began to eat.

"Thank you." Perish took his bowl from the native woman serving them. "Yes, Mother, I have not received a scratch."

"Can you say I didn't see you in white men's clothing?" Beauty met his eyes with the challenge.

Dorothy stopped eating. "For a wedding of the Commander's daughter at Fort Mackinac."

Renault interrupted, "Where is the Bishop?"

It was Ponthe's turn to straighten his back. "He left us."

Beauty pounded the table. The other people in the mess hall turned in their direction. In a harsh whisper Beauty spat, "Wearing Dorothy's pantaloons?"

Dorothy gasped, and Perish took her hand.

"Quiet," Ponthe demanded. "Did they find his body?"

"I did," Renault said. "I buried him at Copper Harbor, where he landed after his fall or jump. His cassock was torn from his trip over the cliff, or from bouncing off the sharp inclines before he hit the rocks below." Renault met Perish's eye. "After I washed them clean, I buried the blue-butterfly trimmed article far away from the crazy Bishop's grave."

"He went mad after a fever." Dorothy cocked her head as if to hear Perish's confirmation.

"Before that," Perish said.

"When?" Dorothy asked him.

"When he stole your pantaloons from the branch they were drying on." Ponthe had answered for him. "Remember, after you fell in the Thames River."

"So, we lost Dasquorant for no reason." Dorothy held her head in her hands.

"Who?" Beauty asked.

"Whipping Stick's nephew of the Seneca tribe," Ponthe answered. "He went south in Michigan hoping to join the Plains Indians.

Perish was still speechless from Dorothy's reaction to the news of the Bishop's death. Her only concern was for Dasquorant who no longer towering over them, paying his respects to Dorothy, and proving his worth as a native hunter. Perish couldn't eat. The food in his mouth tasted like sawdust. Had she loved the real native more than he? After all, his blond hair proved he was at least a half-breed. But a glimmer of renewed hope eased his stomach when he heard Dorothy's next words.

"After the trip," Dorothy asked Beauty, "may we join you on the Raisin River?"

Beauty looked at Perish instead of Dorothy. "What about your schooling? Your trunk will be at Fort Meigs for the stagecoach ride to Philadelphia with the Bishop. The Dominicans are expecting you."

"Not if I'm pregnant."

"Are you?" Beauty asked. Her clear green eyes held a kindly warmth for Perish's intended wife.

"We have not tried," Dorothy said quietly. "Lieutenant Cass stopped our plans for marrying at Fort Mackinac. He said Mother would not approve."

Lieutenant Cass shook his head. "I hope I counseled you correctly."

Beauty nodded. "Sleep separately until you have your mother's approval, Dorothy. Her religion might bar her from seeing you."

"Mother would never shun me." Dorothy smiled at Perish.

Thank you, Orenda, Lord. Perish prayed silently to the one giving God. "Perhaps," he said to his mother, "you could convince Dorothy's mother to bring Father Sebastian to the powwow."

"Good idea." Ponthe patted his son's back.

Finally relaxed enough to continue eating, Perish waited until Dorothy had taken her first bite. Adulthood was a heavier burden than Perish had ever imagined before his vision trip to Copper Harbor. No wonder Ponthe was tiring.

* * *

Like a mother hen, marshalling her chicks, Dorothy noticed where each member of the treaty troupe was housed for the night. Fort Dearborn's number of soldiers had been thinned out to join encampments farther west. Beauty and Renault had no difficulty in prearranging warm housing for each member of the treaty brigade.

Lieutenant Cass, Henry Holt, and Jimmy Sweetwater shared quarters with the remaining soldiers. Renault, Crane, and Flat Belly joined the single men's barracks set aside for the natives during the harsh winter.

The fort's Franciscan priest had returned to Rome, according to Brother Stiles. He assigned Ponthe and Beauty a bedroom in the rectory. When he was informed about the unmarried white couple, he extended his hospitality to them, too.

The monk kept any surprise at the clothing worn by the white travelers hidden as he directed them to their separate bedrooms. "You probably can smell the cabbage soup Mrs. Kerner has cooking." He opened a second floor bedroom door for Beauty and Ponthe. "Ah good, the fire is already warming the room. I'll send our girl, Sally Marksteiner, up with a bowl of the soup for Ponthe." He smiled. "If you want camp news, Sally will have it all."

Any bed off the ground was a luxury. As soon as Perish and Dorothy were inside their separate rooms, they noticed their connecting doors. Dorothy opened the door to find Perish reaching for the handle. Dorothy kissed him long and sweetly. Then she turned away and filled the kettle from the glass water pitcher to provide warm wash water. She jumped into the soft bed patting the empty side next to her for Perish to join her.

A knock on the door interrupted their first heated touch.

"It's me," Sally called.

Dorothy giggled at being caught in bed with Perish.

The girl must have heard. "I'll just leave this bucket of hot water out here. Mrs. Kerner says couples never have enough hot water." She mumbled as she walked away. "I thought that was only for babies."

Perish brought in the bucket, placing it next to the roaring fire. "Mrs. Kerner knows her business."

* * *

In the middle of their familiar embracing ritual, which meant they stayed somewhat clothed, Perish had to admit, white men's bedsprings added a nice dimension. His bride-to-be seemed pleased with the linens more than the springs. He had to tear his pillow from behind her head. "We'll have to go down for dinner, soon," he said.

Dorothy turned her nose up at her buckskin dress. "I wish I had the trunk I sent to Fort Meigs."

"I can ask Renault to retrieve the trunk," Perish said. "He's always ready to get away from civilization."

Beauty was the next to knock, but they had already straightened the coverlet on the bed. "Mother," Perish said. "We're almost ready."

"I'm not worried about being late for dinner." Beauty sat down on the only chair in the room. "Ponthe's very sick."

Perish rushed to her side. "He'll be all right."

"Yes." Beauty looked up at Perish with those beautiful green eyes.

* * *

Dorothy thought Beauty's tears were going to escape, but they did not.

"My biggest problem will be keeping him in bed while his lungs clear." She directed her remarks to Dorothy. "Could you read to him?"

"Of course she will," Perish said.

"Son, I wasn't talking to you." Beauty's shoulders slumped. "Dorothy can speak for herself. I see you're not taking my advice to sleep separately."

"We love each other," Perish said. "We are nourished by each other's touch. We have not mated."

"I'm sorry," Dorothy said. "I agree with Perish. The trip would be more difficult if we were not able to provide some solace for each other. I'm sure Ponthe would be less worn out, if you had accompanied us." Dorothy worried she had stepped over the line in her own defense. "Please forgive me for saying that. Of course, I'd enjoy reading to Ponthe. Lieutenant Cass has four books he's promised to let me read, but we haven't had a moment."

"After supper then," Beauty smiled. "I want to warn you both. Too much privacy when you are this much in love can wear away your best intentions." Beauty stood to leave. "Let my husband, Ponthe Walker, fall asleep before you leave him, Dorothy. He won't be joining us at the table tonight."

The dinner hall of the rectory resembled Fort Detroit's. The shoulder high imported wood paneling was nearly identical, too. But instead of fancy French furniture, the Italian missionaries were provided with a sturdy table and long benches. A carved-back chair sat empty at the head of the table. Brother Stiles sat on one of the benches facing the door.

"Oh, paprika chicken." Dorothy smiled. "My mother cooks this. I miss her."

"I used all her paprika to make red paint for Ponthe's treaty map," Perish told his mother.

Renault was also at dinner. "I've tasted your mother's, Dorothy."

"Which is better?" Brother Stiles winked at Dorothy.

"I'll never tell." Dorothy laughed.

* * *

Perish hadn't heard her laugh for a while. "The trip has been difficult," he said, watching Dorothy across from him.

"I've gotten stronger," Dorothy told Beauty, then apologized. "I'm sorry Ponthe became ill. I didn't notice until after we arrived."

"Tell us about the trip," Brother Stiles said. "Not many travelers are interested in sharing their stories with me."

"Ponthe has gotten the cooperation of the Seneca, Huron, Ottawa, and Delaware to attend the treaty powwow at the end of next summer." Perish hoped he didn't sound worried to his mother.

"I saw a rainbow near the Thames River," Dorothy said. "Before I nearly drowned."

Beauty commented on Perish's conversation. "Ponthe only needs rest."

"For how long?" Renault asked.

"Maybe a month," Beauty stared at Brother Stiles.

"You're welcome to stay." he said, "As I said, not many people want to visit missionaries."

"Have you had many converts?" Dorothy asked politely.

"None." Brother Stiles laughed. "Isn't that marvelous? Perhaps that's why my superior, Abbot Casey, returned to Rome. He said he needed clearer spiritual direction. I have started an Algonquin dictionary, but it's difficult. So many of the aspects of what we white men call cultivated words are unknown to the native society of brothers." he nodded toward Beauty, "and sisters."

Dorothy had stopped eating. "Why did you decide to live as a native?" Dorothy asked Perish's mother.

"I was raised as a native," Beauty said, "like Perish."

"That was 20 years ago." Perish looked directly into Dorothy's eyes. "The white man has taken over more of our world."

The monk didn't lack intelligence. "Dorothy, do want to continue living as a native?"

"Except for no books," Dorothy blurted out. "Living outside seems healthier for children."

"It isn't," Renault said. "I had four children die."

"I didn't know you were married," Perish said.

Renault nodded. "My wife died too, after the last."

"Smallpox," Beauty explained. "My brother, John, died, too."

Renault slumped and Beauty quickly went to his side. "Let's say no more."

"One more sin on our white heads." Brother Stiles bowed his head as if praying for forgiveness.

Perish usually kept his thoughts to himself, saying only half of what he was thinking, but the warm food and satisfying company untied his tongue. "I hope the Great Spirit hears my prayer. I want to provide the best His world has to offer for my wife and children, when I marry."

He had seen the look Dorothy gave her buckskin camp uniform. The sameness of the garment, day after day, ground her down. The lovely sprite of girl he was attracted to, dancing away in her cloud of white petticoats, was gone. The odor of cooked food from every campfire had permeated the dress. The northern freeze left no excuse for not wearing perfume, but the body of the woman he loved smelled only of juniper berries. He didn't hate the smell, but he remembered the constant spring of lilacs that had been her favorite scent. His passion for Dorothy would continue if she wore buckskin or frills, but her spirit lagged behind its highest point by the poverty of her apparel.

"I love my life as a free native, and I hate the white man as much as any native." Perish nodded along with Renault. "But, I need too much from the civilized life to ignore the benefits of living as a white family. A house with fireplaces, windows that open, a sturdy roof against the weather, a library," he nodded toward Dorothy's enormous dark and sultry eyes. "I want it all. I intend to provide everything my family will need."

Perish could feel a tug on his heart as he turned to his mother. "Beauty has seen to my formal education by borrowing every book at Fort Detroit. I'm going to apply for a job as an Indian agent to earn enough money. That way I can watch out for the interests of my native brothers while living as white."

He looked from his mother to his future wife and back again. Neither spoke.

"You're as long-winded as a white man," Renault laughed. "I can tell you that."

Dorothy was silent. Was she was going to cry? "But who will take care of your mother and father?"

"I will," Perish said, putting his arm around his mother's shoulders.

"I'm not living in a house," Beauty said.

"Ponthe already lives in a log cabin," Perish argued.

"Only in the worst winters," Beauty said.

Renault interrupted. "Kdahoi, you are not getting younger. You need to be near your grandchildren...when they appear."

"Yes," Dorothy said. "You do." She looked at Brother Stiles for support, instead of Perish. "But I will not let my children forget the ways of their spiritual fathers. We will learn everything we can from their grandmother while we're at the Raisin River."

Renault stood up to leave. "After I get Dorothy's trunk sent to Fort Detroit, I'm going to start building the house Beauty has always needed."

"Will it be big enough for us all?" Perish asked.

"It will be just like George Washington's farm house," Beauty said.

Brother Stiles laughed nervously. "How many children do you intend to have Dorothy?"

"Six," Dorothy said, "and the first girl will be called Susan. Whipping Stick asked me to remember her."

"Seneca Clan Mothers need remembering," Beauty said. "I said I wasn't living in a house, because I don't have one. You both know as long as I have a roof over my head, my children and grandchildren will, too."

Perish was content. His mother and wife were of the same mind. His children would know where they came from, and he would make sure of their future.

Dorothy turned to the monk. "Let me tell you about my dream. Do you believe in dreams?"

"My husband doesn't," Beauty said, placing her napkin on the table.

"He told us on the trail he believed dreams define the person having the dream," Dorothy said.

Beauty was all ears. Perish knew Ponthe would hear about Dorothy's dream, now.

"He said Perish's vision meant he was ready for a family and children." Dorothy winked at Perish.

"He certainly is." Renault laughed.

"Tell us your dream," Brother Stiles said, probably thinking he was turning the conversation to a safer topic than procreation.

Without hesitation, Dorothy said, "A man was standing at the foot of Copper Harbor."

Perish thought she was going to describe the Bishop's death. Instead, even though he could tell from her swift glance at him she had remembered the reference Copper Harbor had for the rest of them, she continued her dream tale. "I wanted to learn how to swim, since I fell into the Thames River. So there I was, rolling down the hills kicking my hands and feet as I bounced off the cliff. The man below continued to encourage me, 'Yes, that's it. That's how it feels to swim'."

Beauty said, knowing the disasters details. "So you were free...of the man at the bottom of the cliff."

Dorothy blushed. But she was free, free of the constraints the evil man had made on her giving nature.

"I'm glad he's gone," Perish said.

"Me too." Dorothy gave him her angelic yet sensuous smile.

* * *

Ponthe lay too quietly as far as Dorothy was concerned. The room smelled like the mustard plaster Mrs. Kerner had helped Beauty prepare. Steam rose from three kettles boiling in the fireplace. Dorothy helped Ponthe to a sitting position to drink a strong, dark-red tea prescribed by Beauty.

"I think they're trying to kill me." Ponthe smiled weakly.

"They better not," Dorothy said. "Pick a book." She showed him Robinson Crusoe, Rip Van Winkle, Waverly by Walter Scott, and Songs of Innocence by William Blake. The front cover of Robinson Crusoe showed Crusoe in his island garb.

"Is that supposed to be an Indian?" Ponthe pointed at the cover.

"He's an Englishman stranded on an island in the Atlantic."

"Sounds good." Ponthe tried to stifle a cough. "Dorothy, why haven't you and Perish asked Fort Dearborn's missionary to marry you?"

"The abbot is in Rome." Dorothy realized by Ponthe's silence she hadn't explained enough. "Brother Stiles cannot perform sacraments. I mean he can hand out communion wafers, but he can't perform mass or marry anyone. Catholics believe marriage is a sacrament. There are seven."

Ponthe nodded. "Seven is a sacred number to many belief systems. What are the seven Catholic rituals?"

Dorothy tried to recall. "Well there is baptism, confession, communion, confirmation, matrimony, extreme unction. That's only six. I've missed one somewhere. Maybe it is ordination of priests."

"Probably." Ponthe rubbed his throat, as if it hurt to talk. "I assume 'extreme unction' is a death ritual."

"I think it is the final confession." Dorothy opened 'Robinson Crusoe' as she summed up the uncomfortable topic of death's rituals. "communion and then anointing the body with holy water or oils."

Ponthe nodded to her as if he was tired of the subject, or too weary to respond.

So, Dorothy said, "Crusoe opened his Bible at random each day for help, when no other assistance seemed possible."

"How can we, the native people, believe in the Great Spirit?" Ponthe asked. "God has allowed the white man to nearly wipe us from the face of Mother Earth."

Dorothy shook her head. "I know I sound arrogant, Ponthe. But all those hours spent reading in the Jesuit library left me with the same conclusion. God's existence has reason to be doubted. But, I would miss the Lord. I want to love a God who is bigger, wiser than I am. The only thing I've learned is to thank Him when I count my blessings and forgive Him when I can't understand what I consider is His cruelty."

"Forgive God?" Ponthe's eyes were rimmed in red.

Dorothy was sure the cold caused the redness…not any propensity to weep. "Don't you have to forgive Beauty sometimes?" Dorothy closed the book. "Even though I know you love Perish's mother, don't you have to forgive her when you can't understand her?"

"With people, but God?"

"That's how I manage." Dorothy brushed her braids behind her shoulders. "I don't think it's in any theology book."

"Read from Blake." Ponthe's eyes were drooping from the heat or the tea.

Dorothy put Crusoe aside and picked up Blake's book of poems. She found her favorite and began, "It's called 'A Poison Tree:

> *I was angry with my friend:*
> *I told my wrath, my wrath did end.*
> *I was angry with my foe:*
> *I told it not, my wrath did grow.*
>
> *And I watered it in fears,*
> *night & morning with my tears;*
> *and I sunned it with smiles,*
> *and with soft deceitful wiles.'"*

Innocent Ponthe slept.

Chapter Ten

In the Franciscan abbot's study, Perish and Beauty were speaking of spiritual matters at the same time Dorothy and Ponthe were questioning the limits of godly righteousness.

"Did you really see I was injured before you made the trip to Fort Dearborn?" Perish stared into the fire in the grate, trying to imagine his future among the dancing flames.

"I felt it." Beauty hugged herself as if the fire was not emitting enough warmth. "I don't see things."

Perish turned to her. "Could it have been Ponthe's illness you sensed?"

"No, it was your blood." Beauty was sitting in one of the chairs flanking the fireplace. She motioned for Perish to sit down in the other chair.

"Did you notice none of us mentioned Bishop Pascal at dinner?" Perish asked. "Wouldn't Brother Stiles know the Bishop was with us?"

Beauty stroked her brow then patted her black hair. "I think the Jesuits and Franciscans are like different tribes. They don't always talk to each other. I liked the fact that this man, Brother Stiles, leaves the souls of the natives alone."

"Better to let God handle things?"

"Hmmm." Beauty stared into space, listening to something.

Perish found it difficult to sit still. He needed to move to keep up with all the changes in his life. They muddled his mind. He went to the desk and found papers probably written by the abbott as a future sermon. He turned one sheet of paper over and wrote his name, 'Perish North.' Then he switched the order of the names to North Parish. The words spelled and put together in that order sounded like the name of a peaceful community, for a new town on the banks of the Raisin River. "Would you be upset if I changed my name to Parish?" He spelled out his new version for his mother.

"Ponthe named you." Beauty looked at the two names and folded her arms.

The new Parish knew that gesture. She didn't approve. He tried to explain the need to change his name. "Whites will find the word friendlier. Parish means a community of believers. Perish sounds as if I'm destined to die."

Beauty looked skeptical. "No one will hear the difference."

"Ah, but if they see the word spelled out, they will react differently." Parish repeated the two names in his head. The two words did sound the same.

Beauty changed the subject. "What native are you jealous of?"

"Jealous?" Parish strummed his beaded vest. "No one."

"Oh yes," Beauty nodded her head sagely. "A tall Seneca native."

"Dasquorant," Parish admitted.

"He will be returning soon." Beauty clutched her throat. A tear escaped.

Parish's body went on alert. He checked the door and surveyed the curtained windows. "To Fort Dearborn?"

"I don't know." Beauty looked up at him with those green eyes. "Dorothy will be injured."

"Not by Dasquorant." All of Ponthe's doubts about Beauty's ability to see or feel future events surfaced in Parish's mind. But, he remembered Dorothy's voiced concern for Dasquorant.

"The native has feelings for Dorothy?" Beauty was watching his face closely.

"Dasquorant protected her in the past." Parish tried to negate her suggestion in his mind. "...from the Bishop."

Beauty only nodded. "I need to tell you the truth about Ponthe and Renault finding you on the trail."

"What did you lie about?" Parish asked.

"Do you remember the entire story?" Beauty motioned for him to sit down, again.

Parish pulled on his braid to jog his memory. He knew the story of his adoption, didn't he?

* * *

Beauty's green, oval eyes had remained a mystery to all except Renault, who refused to divulge their source to Beauty's Potawatomi brothers and sisters.

"They're her own," Renault had said repeatedly.

Parish was thankful Beauty had accepted him, as Perish, an orphan of domestic strife. He knew the story of Ponthe finding him as a toddler, bruised in the middle of a muddy trail, as if he'd fallen unnoticed from a settler's wagon.

Ponthe had followed the wheel tracks, placing the crying child under the buckboard as if the accident had just happened. Perish's blonde mother tried to hide him among the packed wagon's contents. His cries gave him away. In the morning, Ponthe found him again abandoned in the ditch. Not one to give up easily on humans, Ponthe followed the raging couple for another day. He had hoped their arguments would cease and they would rue the loss of their son. Ponthe had been mistaken.

Renault caught Ponthe absconding into the deep woods with the child. Renault insisted they talk to the couple. Renault stood two heads taller than Ponthe and was twice as wide in the shoulders.

Ponthe drew Renault deeper into the thick woods away from the quarreling couple before he explained why he held a now smiling, yellow-haired baby. "They keep leaving it on the road," Ponthe exclaimed, letting the infant chew on his sleeve's buckskin fringe. "I've returned him twice, but the man beats his wife harder each time."

"We'll see about that." Renault crashed through the trees with Ponthe right behind him.

When the bruised mother spotted the baby, she started to scream cringing in a corner of the wagon bed.

The wife-beater saw an opportunity. "Grab that injun. He raped my wife and stole our baby."

His wife stopped crying.

Renault shook his head. "Naw, that didn't happen." He took the baby from Ponthe and tenderly laid it next to the distraught woman.

She seemed afraid to touch it, but the baby crawled up into her lap. The babe pulled the faded fabric of her bodice to one side so he could nurse.

"Cover yourself, you whore," the husband yelled.

Renault put his heavy hand on Ponthe's shoulder where the muscles twitched in anger. "Take yourselves off now," Renault said as he pushed Ponthe into the woods.

Once they were out of earshot, Renault said. "That's far enough. Let's circle back to make sure the child is safe."

They could hear the women's cries before they could see the savage attack. The madman of a husband was stabbing his wife's breasts. The baby lay limp on the ground, a gash where his head had hit a rock. Renault lifted the man off his feet with one hand on his throat. When the man dropped his knife, his wife stuck it in his chest and turned it. Renault didn't let go until the man stopped kicking. By then, the wife was close to death from the multiple stab wounds. Renault threw the body of the husband into the woods.

"Leave them," Ponthe said, pulling his friend away. "Someone will find them."

Then they heard the cry. The baby was sitting up rubbing his head and whimpering softly.

The mother called to it, "Baby."

Ponthe brought the child to its mother for a final kiss.

"Don't let him see the blood," she said, struggling to cover her wounds. "Keep him safe. That animal was not his father." She seemed to gain strength with the sight of her child. "The Potawatomi Indian, North, was his father. Cut a lock of my hair, so he knows his mother was white."

Renault cut a long golden ringlet from her hair.

"Promise...," was all the woman could whisper.

Ponthe and Renault nodded their agreement to the deadening eyes.

Renault had swooped up the child as he raced to join Ponthe away from the domestic carnage.

"Take him," Ponthe said as they neared a clearing.

Renault had frowned down at the child, who interpreted the scowl as danger and began to wail.

"You found him first." The tough trapper gave the screaming toddler to his friend.

Ponthe nestled the child in the crook of his arm. The babe quieted as he re-found the chewed fringe on Ponthe's sleeve. "I'll call him Perish," Ponthe said.

"Yep," Renault agreed, happy to have the matter settled. "He nearly did."

* * *

Back in the Fort Dearborn study, Beauty said, "I told you the story each year."

Of course, she didn't tell Parish the part about the mutilation and murders. Renault filled him in when she wasn't around. Beauty had shown him the long, silky tresses of yellow hair that Renault had cut after his birth mother begged Ponthe to keep the child safe.

"Where is the lie?" Parish asked. "My mother was white."

"Renault did not come upon Ponthe by accident." Beauty said. "I'm telling you this now, because of what you will face." She bowed her head and added, "Shortly, too soon, too soon." Then Beauty reached for Parish's hand. "I know Dorothy thinks our way of life, living in the open, free of greed, directly under the Great Spirit's mercy, is the best way to raise children."

Someone important was going to be ripped from his life. "My Dorothy loves me."

"You need to know, now. I am your blood relative too, Parish. I am your father's sister."

Parish examined Beauty's face, her green eyes, her strong cheek bones, her black hair. Why did she seem intent on telling him this tall tale?

Beauty seemed to sense his disbelief. "Renault arranged my adoption by the Potawatomi with my younger brother, John Perry North. He was your father. Your mother was enamored of the romance of native life, just as Dorothy is. Your mother was married when she pursued my brother, thinking he was a member of the Potawatomi tribe. When John died of smallpox, your mother was already pregnant by him, so she returned to her husband. That's why Renault was following them. I asked him to find out where she settled to keep in touch with you, someday. Remember when Renault told you his family was wiped out?"

Parish's hand strayed to one of his blond braids.

Beauty stood and took Parish's hand away from his hair. "I told you then that my brother, John, died too. But I asked Renault not to say any thing more. Do you remember the conversation?"

Parish recalled Renault's statement, but he had been so concerned about his decision of how to live with Dorothy as his bride that he hadn't listened to Beauty's comment. "I'm sorry. I should have asked more about your brother, my father, at the time."

Beauty sat back down. "I was glad you didn't at the time. Ponthe might not have understood. As children, Renault dyed our hair black so the tribe would accept us more readily. John's hair was originally as blond as was mine, but our mother's was red. She had green eyes, too. I keep my hair dark even now, or you would see your old aunt's white hairs."

His mother, his aunt, might actually be speaking the truth now. Parish first saw the tallest native he had ever met. Dasquorant had dismissed Dorothy and himself as white. When Parish considered the fact that Dorothy might evaluate Dasquorant's native skills against his own, he had worried. If it hadn't been for Dasquorant, would he have made claim to Dorothy as soon as he did? Parish had known even then no good would come from meeting the man. No good. "And Ponthe knows I'm entirely of white blood?" Parish asked.

"No, dear." Beauty didn't meet his eyes. "Neither Renault nor I had the courage to tell your adopted father that I was not at least half Potawatomi and that your father was entirely white."

"I should tell them." Parish said. "They need to know. They both love me because they think I have native blood in my veins."

"Your heart is more important than your bloodline." Beauty faced the fire, smoothing her hair.

"That's exactly what Ponthe said in Washington." Parish thought he saw Beauty's shoulders shudder. Was she so unsure of Ponthe's affection, she needed to maintain this lie. Parish berated himself. He wasn't prepared to accept Dorothy's rejection either. "If you're not ready to share the truth with Ponthe," Parish sighed. "I can wait to tell Dorothy."

Beauty turned, stood, and placed her hand on his shoulder. "I will never forget this gift of trust, Parish. I'm too old to find anyone but Ponthe to love me."

Parish was certain beyond question, in his heart, that Ponthe's affection would not change for his aunt; but he wasn't that convinced of Dorothy's continued affection.

* * *

The weeks dragged by. Dorothy read to Ponthe each night until his coughing became too disruptive for him to listen. Beauty said it was a good sign, the pestilence was leaving his lungs. Dorothy didn't like the look of Ponthe. His coughs racked his body, left him listless and aching, but his fever was gone.

Embracing her intended each night was all well and good, but with nothing to set his mind to, Parish as he insisted on being called, resorted to quarreling with Dorothy about unimportant things, like the change of his name from 'Perish' to 'Parish.' No one heard the change in spelling and Dorothy couldn't really see how anyone would notice the difference.

One night when Parish had left her exhausted from his insistent conversation, she felt unwilling to hear his next words. He kissed her eyes. Her mouth was swollen from his rapt kisses. She brushed Parish's lips with her fingertips, remembering the sensations that had rioted through her.

Parish kissed her fingertips and asked, "Do you really believe we will stay together forever?"

"Until death," she promised.

"What happened to forever?" He stroked his beaded vest, which Dorothy knew meant hours of further discussions. "Forever goes beyond death."

"Okay, forever." Dorothy started to drift into the weightlessness of sleep.

"So you wouldn't marry if I died?"

Dorothy rubbed her eyes. "You're bored and trying to start trouble."

"I'm not bored," Parish said. "Boredom is when you die while you're still alive."

"For me boredom feels like contentment." She snuggled down into the lovely, fresh smelling pillows on the bed.

Parish shook her. "Would you marry?"

"Yes," she said, taking the bait. "I would. I think I would enjoy being married."

* * *

Parish stomped out of the room into the adjacent one. He didn't close the connecting door. Maybe he should go back to the silence of his vision quest. Beauty was right. Dorothy had injured him by promising to marry him. Her ideas often clashed with his. Like the law. Dorothy appreciated it as a refuge of society for those who were treated badly. Parish perceived it as a white man's tool to steal land and restrict freedom.

He'd paraphrased the Bible to her, "When Moses demanded the ten commandments from God, God was reluctant to give them. He kept asking Moses, 'Why do the people want them? As soon as I make a law, they will lose no time in breaking all of them'."

"What are you telling me?" she'd asked. "Which commandment are you planning to break?"

Maybe there should have been a law about not staying in one place for too long. Parish wondered how he was going to start a life with a family if he was so easily bored...indoors. Marriage certainly wouldn't solve every dilemma. It was a joy to be near Dorothy; but that didn't mean there were fewer problems. Sufficient unto the day is the trouble thereof. Was that a Bible verse?

If they hadn't met at Fort Detroit, Dorothy might have remained with her mother. Parish might have pursued the native life in peace. But now he had responsibilities: a promised wife who didn't want to leave him. He smiled. Dorothy loved him.

* * *

The weather in Illinois was worse than Sturgeon Bay's. At least there the Delaware had constructed stone wigwams. In Illinois, the wind hit you from all sides at the same time. Parish missed the tranquility of his Raisin River home, away from the constant wind.

Potawatomi families gathered in and around Fort Dearborn. Behind the western wall of the fort, away from the wicked winds off Lake Michigan, wigwams and teepees appeared overnight. Lake Erie winds had to blow pretty hard across Lake St. Clair for the Fort Detroit dwellers to notice. Its western wall, in the lee of the winds, was a popular place for the natives to camp. But at Fort Dearborn, ropes had to be tied between the eastern lakeshore trees for those on foot to stay upright in the gale-force blasts of wind. And behind the fort, the bone-chilling winds off the plains slammed into the natives.

Flat Belly brought the new arrivals to Parish to be checked off the list that Beauty and Ponthe had provided. By the 15th of February, 31 families were counted.

Alexander and Richard Godfrey, the adopted white children of the tribe, were housed in the rectory basement. Parish found the two orphans gravitated toward Jimmy Sweetwater and Henry Holt. Lieutenant Cass kept an eye on them, and the teenagers were finally moved to the barracks.

Evening meals at the rectory included native families that Brother Stiles invited to his abbott's table. Crane attended as the interpreter. One evening, Waninsheway called White Elk, a sturdy warrior, and his father interrupted their meal.

Brother Stiles immediately called for Sally and Mrs. Kerner. "Put more water in the soup ladies, we have more company."

Instead, the two broke the news. "No more will come." Missensusai called Mensend, who was White Elk's father, folded his arms.

Then the younger White Elk added, "We are gathered for Ponthe."

Beauty's head bowed for Parish to answer. "My adopted father is too ill in his throat to speak to you all. I have the treaty map and his instructions. Do I have your permission to speak in his stead?"

Mensend asked. "Can you answer all the questions from the tribal leaders?"

"If I cannot," Parish readily admitted, "I will consult with Ponthe."

"We expect Ponthe will be well enough to continue the treaty trip to St. Louis and Fort Wayne at the end of February," Beauty added.

"Wawcacee named Full Moon and Medouin, that you call Corn," White Elk spoke slowly for the monk, who wrote down each name. "Wish for the Midewiwin Society to have a Dream Dance before we hear about the white men's next movements."

Parish cocked his head to ask Brother Stiles' approval.

"Oh, that's fine. Would I be able to attend?" the monk asked White Elk. "I will try to write down all I see, so that your children's children will remember the dance."

"The dirt floor of the soldier's mess hall would be best for the winter dance," Parish suggested. "The entrance faces east."

White Elk and Mensend bowed and left the room.

"Eat, eat," Brother Stiles excitedly directed his guests.

Parish resumed his seat at the table. A bead fell from his vest into his cold soup. As he touched his shoulder, an entire string of beads let go scattering over the table and floor.

Beauty went to him and tied a knot in the offending row of decorations on his vest.

He wondered if his aunt thought the breaking of the string a bad sign. Was the accident further negation of his right to call himself a native?

* * *

Later, Beauty knocked on the bedroom door of her nephew's room at the rectory.

Dorothy invited her in. "I'm sorry. Parish is down with Lieutenant Cass hanging the map in the soldiers' mess hall."

"I wanted to speak to you," Beauty said. "I have a gift for you for the rest of the trip down south." She placed a square package wrapped in a red army blanket on their bed.

"A present." Dorothy clapped her hands. "Should I wait for Parish to return to open it?"

"It's only for you," Beauty said.

Dorothy unwrapped the folds of the blanket. Inside was a new buckskin dress. Pleats were inserted in the sides with delicate beadwork down the edge of each pleat.

"It's beautiful."

Beauty untied the waist ties of the garment and shook it out. "After you marry, when the babies grow bigger you can adjust the strings for more room."

Dorothy's world expanded beyond the possibilities contained in any pleated buckskin. "Have you seen our future?"

"In a dream," Beauty said matter-of-factly. "You can name the boy Renault."

Dorothy's disappointment was measurable. "A boy."

"No," Beauty said. "Twins, Susan and Renault."

Weeping with joy, Dorothy hugged her mother-in-law. "My mother?" she choked out.

"I'll see her, when I visit Fort Detroit...." Beauty touched Dorothy's forehead. "...as soon as Ponthe is able to travel with you."

Dorothy wanted to embrace the woman longer, but Beauty turned away. "Does Parish know that when we marry, we will have twins?"

"Not yet, but he might see more visions by the end of the Dream Dance."

Dorothy saw the smile and comprehended why her future mother-in-law was called Beauty. The smile lit not just her face and eyes, but her being seemed lighter...as if she would float away with delight.

"I'll be married into a magical family," Dorothy, the future mother-to-be, said. How did Beauty know she would birth twins?

* * *

The rough tables in the huge eating hall were pushed to the walls. Dorothy noted that most of the Potawatomi children were seated on the tables to get a better view of the dancers. Dorothy and Beauty sat with Brother Stiles.

When he entered the hall, Parish carried a long wooden elk whistle decorated with eagle feathers that White Elk had given him. He began the Dream Dance with a series of harmonic calls that sounded almost like a bugle.

Flat Belly, White Elk, Full Moon, Corn, and Wynemakowo, called Trout, entered the packed hall. They wore porcupine vests and eagle feather roaches in their hair. Elaborate feather bustles decorated their backs.

Brother Stiles wrote furiously in his notebook.

Each dancer was fantastically painted from head to foot. A banner of shell work crossed White Elk's chest. Brass sleigh bells encircled the knees and ankles of the other dancers. Flat Belly held a staff topped with a buffalo horn spoon. Full Moon's staff with a saw-toothed wooden handle was wrapped with leather lashes. Four more natives manned the drums.

Parish spoke before the drums began. "My father, Ponthe Walker, would like the Algonquin Potawatomi to listen to his favorite Iroquois parable before we start the Dream Dance."

The men sat in a semicircle facing the east door.

Parish began. "Hiawatha dreamt the Five-Nation treaty for the Iroquois. With his help, the Mohawk, Seneca, Huron, Delaware, and the Erie lived in peace after many years of struggle and bloodshed. George Washington based the Declaration of Independence on Hiawatha's wisdom.

"In Hiawatha's dream, ducks lifted the lake so that Hiawatha could cross on dry land. He found shells in the lakebed, which he strung on thrushes to make the first wampum list of tribal history. Each night Hiawatha picked up the wampum strings and repeated the plea for condolence, hoping someone would hear. Deganawida, the incarnation of mercy, a healing spirit in human form, taught Hiawatha how to allay passions with solemn mourning rituals. Hiawatha was able to reason once more with himself and others.

"Hiawatha consoled those who had lost family in the wars with the shell words to lift away the darkness of revenge. Prisoners and the enemies' orphans were adopted into families to replace lost members...as the Potawatomi adopted the Godfrey brothers. We wish to inspire ourselves in this coming dance with inner harmony to face the outward strife caused by living among the whites."

Parish blew the whistle, and the drummers of the water drums started the rhythm. Women relatives gave intermittent high-pitched trills, made by vibrating the tongue rapidly against the roof of the mouth. Each dancer had his own routine, not repeated by any of the other dancers. The bells and incessant beat of the drum and the elk whistle moved the dancers to increasingly rapid movements. Sometimes one dancer would sing, sometimes another. Still they circled around and around, working themselves into a frenzy, then into a near reverie of exhaustion, but they continued to move.

Parish joined the dancers. His flanks were naked beneath the swinging breach cloth. The dance leggings he wore stopped above his knees. As the dance progressed, he shed his shirt but not his vest or brass gorget. Only his hair let others know that this spirited dancer was not completely one of them.

The hum of the rhythmic noise, the throbbing of the dirt floor, the heat emanating from the dancers combined with the aroma of dust and sweat. Dorothy's nerves reacted as if Parish were touching her: warming her blood, easing all her nerves. She felt herself nodding off.

The drums ceased abruptly, bringing Dorothy to her feet.

Brother Stiles continued to write down his impressions.

Parish stood to speak, as the dreaming dancers sat. "Each Potawatomi who travels to the Maumee River Rapids will receive $1,300 dollars each year for fifteen years. The Godfrey brothers will receive 640 acres to build a trading post and schools. Any Potawatomi brother who does not attend the powwow will not receive their allotted 640 acres. In return, the reservations in Illinois will be ceded back to the Great White Father."

White Elk stood to speak "Before we harvest our first crop of corn on the new land, the white settlers will come,"

Parish didn't have the heart to dispute him. "Ponthe told the Seneca we must act like trained bears in the feeding pits. Our families will need to eat today and tomorrow."

Hiawichemon, named Hiya, spoke next, "It is good for you to try to teach us not to hate the white man." He said no more.

* * *

Ten days later, Parish found that the Potawatomi had disappeared as quietly as they had assembled. Flat Belly, Crane, and Beauty said their good-byes to the treaty travelers before leaving for Fort Detroit.

"What do we tell Father Sebastian when we arrive at Fort Detroit?" Flat Belly asked Ponthe, who had been well enough to eat with them for a couple of weeks.

"About Bishop Pascal?" Crane added.

"That he walked away from us." Ponthe stood but kept his fist on the table.

Parish gave his opinion, "Wait until Renault returns to the fort with Dorothy's trunk. He'll have to explain why Dorothy decided not to go with the Bishop to the school in Washington."

"Bad idea." Beauty shook her head. "Father Sebastian knows Renault was with me when I left to meet you. As soon as we get inside the gates of Fort Detroit, I will tell the priest."

Ponthe rubbed his smooth chin. "Yes, wife, you must."

Parish took note of the lesson in husbandry.

"Try not to tell them that Dasquorant was with us," Ponthe added.

"What if the Seneca inquire?" Beauty touched her husband's shoulder.

Ponthe resumed his seat, as if tired by the contention. "Tell them he was well when he left us for the plains."

* * *

Illinois River to St. Louis

In early March, Ponthe had recovered sufficiently to take charge of buying the two river canoes needed to travel down the Illinois River to St. Louis. They would portage the canoes until they reached the Illinois River. Once they were launched, Lieutenant Cass, Henry Holt, and Jimmy Sweetwater traveled behind the canoe of Ponthe, Dorothy, and Parish.

Dorothy had not informed Parish of Beauty's prediction of a twin pregnancy. She didn't want him to dispute the hope of future twins she held close to her heart. Ponthe might deny Beauty's words, too. Then what would the fates bring but disaster. Dorothy would never again have a chance to see the boundaries of the Old

Northwest. With two children to raise, there would be no free time to explore more of the world.

On the second day, the Illinois River was running high with floods from the northern thaws. Trees and debris battled with the canoes for their rights of passage. The sun grew warm, and each mile of river south brought more signs of the greening of spring.

At one point where the river was relatively clear, Dorothy's heart felt it might burst with happiness.

A Catholic liturgy song of joy lifted from her soul to God,

> *"Come Holy Ghost, Creator blest,*
> *and in our hearts take up Thy rest.*
> *Come with Thy grace and Heavenly aid*
> *to fill the hearts which Thou hast made..."*

Lieutenant Cass sang the familiar Catholic repeated verse with her, to fill the hearts which Thou hast made...."

Ponthe couldn't keep an ironic tone out of his response, "I take it you two are happy with the weather."

Parish laughed, and Henry Holt chimed in with his southern farmer's cackle.

Dorothy summoned her courage. She sat between Ponthe and Parish in the canoe. Maybe they wouldn't pay close attention. The flood's debris was increasing again, keeping them busy enough. She spoke as quietly as she could, "Beauty says I will conceive twins after I marry."

Ponthe continued to paddle as did Dorothy.

* * *

Parish automatically put his paddle into the canoe, lest he drop it. "Twins?"

Dorothy grinned at Parish as if handing him a bag of gold, then pushed her paddle against a floating tree.

"Ponthe," he called, "Will she be safe?"

"From what?" Ponthe and Dorothy said in unison, mocking him.

He could feel his anger rising. "Why didn't you share my mother's prediction sooner?"

Dorothy's voice fell from the happier tone. "I was afraid you wouldn't believe your mother."

Wrong again, he'd said the wrong thing at the wrong time, again. He'd make it up to her. He turned around and yelled at Lieutenant Cass and the other boat. "I'm going to be a father of twins!"

A huge cheer went up in the other boat, frightening a flock of migrating cranes from the treetops. Parish was pleased with himself. He pointed to the birds. "A good sign."

Dorothy said as quietly as she had when she announced the impending parenthood, "Their names will be Renault and Susan."

Parish was silent. He was not going to fall into a word trap for a second time. "Twins." That sounded safe to his ears. His lovely bride would some day bear him children.

"What do you think of the names?" she asked.

"I like them," Ponthe cued Parish to follow the right line of conversation to stay out of trouble.

"Me too." Parish grinned from ear to ear.

Dorothy gave him her approving smile. "Your mother liked the names, too. She had a dream."

Parish only nodded an agreement.

Ponthe didn't fare as well. "Of course she did."

"Are you implying that she didn't have a dream?" Dorothy was definitely not happy, now.

Ponthe reached behind him and patted Dorothy's knee. "Don't get mad at me little mother. I'll be the grandfather. If Beauty had a dream, Beauty had a dream."

With sarcasm dripping into the river, Dorothy asked, "And what does it tell you about her?"

"Why that Beauty wants to be a grandmother, quickly." Ponthe began to paddle in earnest.

Parish didn't agree with his father about the ineffectiveness or guarantees of dreams. Part of him wanted Dorothy to have twins, eventually. There would be one baby for each of them to hold. The worrying part of him concentrated on the added responsibility.

"Plenty of time to plan for them," Dorothy reassured them, continuing to paddle.

There was the fact that Parish didn't yet have a job as an Indian Agent. He began to paddle in concert with Dorothy and Ponthe. Until money came in regularly, they would have no choice but to live as part of the tribe at the Raisin River home of his mother.

He could do that. No problem.

__Chapter Eleven__

St. Louis

The twentieth of April brought heavy weather to St. Louis.
From the speed of the dark green clouds rushing toward the
Mississippi River, Dorothy judged the storm advancing on the flat
western horizon was two miles away from them. The bright white
thunder caps rose into the stratosphere while continuous thunder
warned of the Almighty's power. Lightning struck the ground
repeatedly on each side of the river.

Ponthe directed them to beach the canoes on the western shore.
A sand bar had eaten into the black earthen bank providing a natural
break from the winds.

"Look!" Henry screamed.

Coming at them from the west, a twister with a base as wide as
Fort Dearborn hung in the clouds.

"Under the canoes," Ponthe shouted. "Hold on to each other and
the braces."

Both he and Parish had their arms around Dorothy. Their
shoulders where hooked in the canoe. Sand and water whipped the
shore. Their backs to the wind, they faced the black wall of the
riverbank.

"Will we die?" Dorothy asked.

"Not without a fight," Parish said, kissing her face where his
head touched it.

The howling winds stopped.

Ponthe pushed the canoe up to look.

Above them, Dorothy beheld the wide mouth of the tornado. It
seemed to draw the very breath from her lungs.

Then the black, revolving horror was gone over their heads to
the east. The roar of destruction was deafening. The howl and the
ear-splitting noise sounded as if all the buildings in East St. Louis
were being torn off their foundations and then slammed into the
ground. Trees and bushes still traveled over their heads into the
tornado's vortex.

"Make it stop," Jimmy Sweetwater yelled, "Make it stop."

Lieutenant Cass lifted the canoe as Ponthe and Parish had. Dorothy could now hear the screams of injured people.

"We have to help them," Lieutenant Cass said.

Parish had climbed up the bank above them. "Fires are starting."

"It's the end of the world," Jimmy shouted.

Lieutenant Cass cuffed him. "Steady, boy."

The six apprehensive travelers crossed the river, stowed their gear under the canoes and then moved up the east bank into what remained of St. Louis. They walked down a cleanly swept boulevard the tornado had ripped out of the town. Children were calling for parents. Neighbors were pulling neighbors out from under wrecked buildings.

Ponthe shook his head in dismay. "Let's rescue as many as we can."

"The fires are coming this way," a bystander screamed.

Ponthe took Dorothy's arm. "The fires will run east with the wind. We're safe."

She didn't feel safe. She wanted her mother. Jimmy was shaking. Henry tried to calm him down.

"To work, boys," Parish called.

Dorothy joined them as they pushed aside lumber. Underneath the debris, a family emerged from their root cellar. Five children, all girls, a mother and father. All safe.

A mounted troop of ragtag Indian scouts raced toward them. Dorothy counted a dozen riders. Each pair of hands was heaven sent.

"When did you expect the Shawnee?" Parish asked his father.

Ponthe greeted the Shawnee brigade. "No time for formal greetings, Quitewe."

The men dismounted and set to work. Dorothy counted three army-officer uniforms. The new rescuers worked side-by-side with them, following the calls for help, digging until a bloodied hand could be grasped or a frightened baby handed up.

The sun was setting when Dorothy relinquished a child into the grimy arms of its smiling mother. They worked until they could no longer see their own hands in the gathering dark. Along the edge of the path that the tornado had scoured through the town, bodies were lined up. Their faces were covered with torn blankets or their own shirts or skirts. Everything smelled like the river mud mixed with soot and raw meat.

Ponthe called a halt. "Back to the river. Dorothy, could we have cold biscuits and coffee. We'll come back in the morning."

"We'll join your camp at daybreak," Quitewe said. "It's a sad time."

The Shawnee gathered their horses and rode east down the path of destruction reaped by the tornado. As the six treaty-travelers turned west toward the river, Lieutenant Cass pulled his pistol out and pointed at a shadow or a man running across their path to the river.

"Looters," Parish explained to Dorothy.

Thieves at a time like this? Dorothy found it difficult to believe. "Isn't God's disaster enough?"

"An opportunity for some," Ponthe sadly admitted.

"Hard to have morals when poverty beckons," Henry whispered.

Lieutenant Cass stood first guard at their camp that night, Ponthe and then Parish took their turns.

* * *

Jimmy Sweetwater had his bedroll as far removed from the campsite as he dared. He opened his second bottle of whiskey. Jimmy liked the excitement of storms. Every cell in his body felt alive...and there was this sudden bounty of firewater. A rough hand tore the bottle from his grasp. Jimmy thought he was seeing an alcohol-summoned ghost in the flickering campfire light.

The Seneca, Dasquorant, towered over him.

"Ponthe!" Jimmy called as loudly as his frozen throat would allow. After too many moments had hung in the soft spring night, Jimmy took a relaxed breath.

"Calm yourself," Ponthe said, his hand on the shaking lad's shoulder.

"I came behind the wind," Dasquorant said.

* * *

Parish didn't feel as welcoming as he should when Ponthe brought Dasquorant into the camp's circle. Beauty's words of warning rang in his ear. Dorothy would be injured. Before he could voice his concerns to Dorothy, who was busy at first light with her cooking pots, the Shawnee, who had helped with the rescue efforts, arrived.

Ponthe named the faces that had worked until nightfall with them. Wearing the army officer jackets were Quitawepea or Captain Lewis the peace chief, Quietewe or War Chief, and Cheacksca or Captain Tom.

Parish recognized a few of the Washington delegation. Wawalthethaka or Captain Reed gave the names of three other men in his tribe, "and the white man called Othawakeseka or Yellow Feather.

Yellow Feather shook Parish's hand. Both of them had the yellow hair of the white man. "Here are three more of my dangerous brothers," Yellow Feather smiled but did not laugh. "Shenenstu or Big Snake, Gateweekesa, or Black Hook, and Biesaka or Wolf."

Big Snake strolled up face-to-face Dasquorant. They matched each other's height. "What Huron servant is this?" he asked.

Dasquorant pushed Big Snake's chest at the implied derision. "Seneca, you Shawnee fool."

Knives gleamed in the early light.

Dorothy approached the two with bowls of porridge. "Breakfast is ready, if you two will trade your knives for spoons."

Beauty was right. Dorothy was going to get herself killed. Both men sheathed their knives but not their glares. They wolfed down the piping hot cereal. Parish's stomach growled. There hadn't been time for much of an evening meal after they'd worked like dogs to rescue as many people as they could.

Ponthe spoke. "Dasquorant has offered to share our travels at his Clan Mother's spiritual request. A dream pointed him in the direction of the great wind, which destroyed many homes of the white man. Now he will accompany us to the Maumee Rapids."

The Shawnee War Chief, Quitewe, spoke. "Your brothers are our brothers."

Big Snake set his empty bowl close to Dorothy's kettle.

"You're welcome," she said, as if trying to teach him reverse manners.

The large native resembled a prancing spring stallion, as he kicked a rolling log back into the fire. Big Snake lingered around Dorothy too long, as far as Parish was concerned. Even Dasquorant found it necessary to flank Dorothy and resume his glare at Big Snake.

Parish called her, "Wife, bring me another bowl."

Ponthe looked at him in surprise then assessed the scene.

Dorothy gracefully brought him a second bowl of porridge. "Thanks," she whispered.

At least Dorothy hadn't scolded him for calling her 'wife.' But the word rolled off his tongue so easily; as if this beautiful damsel busy with her camp chores was already a partner of his. Parish's heart swelled to think Dorothy had just as easily accepted the word. They were one. Even if they had not consummated a sexual act, even if no religious ceremony had been performed, in their hearts they were already one. Please, Great Spirit, help me protect Dorothy. Parish knew he would lay down his life twice for her; because he couldn't imagine a life without Dorothy's companionship.

Ponthe moved next to Quitewe. "While my son finishes his breakfast, we will have time to go over the land allocations."

Quitewe nodded and motioned for Big Snake to join his shorter warrior friends, Black Hook and Wolf. The Shawnee prepared to listen.

Yellow Feather came to Parish and Dasquorant's side. "Quick thinking," he said. "We've had some trouble keeping those three in check."

Ponthe began the hated treaty words. "The 23 Shawnee at Hog Creek will receive 24 square miles. Wapghkonetta, the village of 148 natives, will receive $1,118 this year and money due for land from any former treaties. After the treaty is signed at Maumee Rapids, $3,956.50 will be paid plus $2,000 per year, forever, along with ten square miles for a council house. The Delaware, Hembis petitioners, now living at Wapaghkenetta will receive $358.50. Children of the Chief Sapmageladbe, Captain Logan, who died in service will also receive $358.50 each. The number of parcels of land, 640 acres, divided at Maumee Rapids, will depend on how many Shawnee attend to sign for the land."

Captain Lewis, their Peace Chief answered, "None will fail to gather."

"Now we must give aid to our helpless white brothers," Ponthe said. "Jimmy Sweetwater, Dorothy, and Henry will stay in camp."

Parish knew the reason. The younger boys and Dorothy didn't need to see the carnage they would find this day as bodies and parts of bodies were recovered in the debris from the tornado's aftermath.

* * *

Dorothy set the boys to work around the camp. She had anticipated spending a night with Parish under a roof as they had approached St. Louis. Now every available bed would be used for the devastated town's injured.

"The Shawnee will probably join us for supper," she explained, when she asked Jimmy to use the net to catch fish.

The poor boy had a hang-over from the whiskey Dasquorant confiscated. Dorothy couldn't remember Jimmy being separated from the rescue crew long enough to find bottles of whiskey. He was a sly one.

"Henry, fill all the pots for me, and keep the fire going. I'm going to bathe." Dorothy's monthly cycle required the bathing ritual. She had run across the books borrowed from Lieutenant Cass in her luggage.

When she returned to the campfire, she called Jimmy. "Any luck?"

"The fish are angry," Jimmy said chopfallen.

"No one is angry with you, but you," Dorothy told him. "It's going to be a long afternoon. Why don't I read to you both for a while and then you can try again."

"I like to be read to," Henry said, sitting as close as possible.

Dorothy gave the boy's dirty hair a yank. "Go jump in the river with Jimmy, scrub your head, and I'll read to you when you get back."

Dorothy tried to turn her face away from the sight.

Jimmy and Henry shed their clothes as they ran, jumping and cavorting like young lambs until they dove into the refreshing river. When they dressed, they shook water from their hair like wet dogs.

Dorothy waited for them to sit before she began Crusoe, "I was born in the Year 1632, in the City of York, of a good Family, tho' not of that Country, my Father being a Foreigner of Bremen, who settled first at Hull. He got a good Estate by Merchandise, and leaving off his Trade, lived afterward at York, from whence he had married my mother...."

The young men dozed in the warm sun. The storm had brought sultry weather, and the clear sky denied any responsibility for the dark terrors of the night before. The evening's shocks had been hard on their sensibilities. Everyone's nerves were frazzled. Of course,

Jimmy's short excursion into alcohol had been foiled, but he still suffered.

Dorothy stopped reading and the boys slept on.

Dorothy peeled all the vegetables she possessed to throw into the pot. Moving the bubbling brew to the edge of the fire, she rested her head just for a minute on her blanket folded on top of her back pack. The emotions of fear, gladness at rescuing the trapped, and sadness at those beyond help exhausted her normally resilient body.

No noise woke her, but a feeling of doom washed over her as she spied the rescuers bringing a body back to camp. Dorothy didn't know how long she had slept.

"Boys," Dorothy called softly, not wanting the dozing young men to become as frightened as she was. Dasquorant and Parish laid Ponthe's body down next to the campfire. When Dorothy tried to disturb the blanket wrapped around Ponthe's head, Parish removed her hands. Lieutenant Cass, the boys, and the Shawnee gathered around the fallen leader.

"Tell me," Dorothy whispered.

Black Snake moved away from the others toward her. "I meant to harm Dasquorant, but Ponthe stepped between us." A haunted look overcame his face.

Dasquorant spoke softly. "The peacemaker died trying to keep peace, because of me."

Parish didn't speak. He sat next to the body, holding Ponthe's hand, comforting Ponthe for his trip into the land of dead.

Dorothy's insides seemed to collapse. Her mind was stunned into silence. She came to herself, seated on the opposite side of Ponthe, holding his other hand. Now, whom would they go to for wisdom? Ponthe was the only male parent she had ever known. Sixteen was too early to be orphaned from someone who loved her as his daughter. He wanted to be a grandfather of her children. Now they would never know the great man, who had guided so many lives through this transitional time in history. The world was of less worth now.

Silence reigned among the people on the shore as they watched the river moved on between the banks.

* * *

In the mind of Parish, Ponthe's peaceful spirit whispered goodbye. "Blame no one. Keep on the treaty trail. Finish my task."

Parish didn't shed tears on the outside. But beneath his skin, his blood turned to fire. His heart seemed to fill his chest. He could hear the pounding in his ears. His brain felt cold, his tongue dry. A stunned confusion clouded his mind.

One moment alive, dead the next. No one could prepare sufficiently for death. There were no defenses on earth.

'Great Spirit,' Parish prayed silently, 'shall I die? My heart beats through lead, my head feels like a prison of pain, my limbs are weak, my belly a knot. If I stop breathing, who will watch over my Dorothy? Protect me, Lord, from my own hand of destruction.'

A great wave of consolation encompassed him. Ponthe's spiritual arms enclosed him as when he was a young boy. Perhaps God was in his heaven, but all was not right in the world. Ponthe lay dead from a senseless, violent action. Dead at his feet.

Parish needed to face reality with as much courage as he possessed. Still he felt negated, less of who he was by the loss of his father. The lie of being native made him feel invisible. What was God thinking, to make him white? Now Ponthe would know in the spirit world his adopted son had a white mother and a white father, Beauty's brother. All Parish loved as a boy was native. Now all that remained in his life, his wife-to-be, was white. His grief included the tragedy of losing his native heritage. Even as whites tried to wipe away any trace of the Iroquois or the Algonquin in the Old Northwest, God had taken Parish's treasured native parent. Ponthe's voice would not be heard again. By listening to his raging soul, Parish had somehow stilled the storm within himself. The silence and peace calmed him further. How long would the pain continue?

* * *

Dorothy's tears were wetting the front of her dress. She didn't try to stop them. Mostly she identified the self-pity flooding her being. She was crying for her mother, not seeing her. And, she was crying for Beauty, for not knowing that her life mate was dead. She was crying for Parish who had lost the only father he had every known. Dorothy cried again for the lost father figure she had found in Ponthe, for his gentleness. Mostly she mourned the loss of his acceptance of her into his native world. Who would guide them now? Who would comfort her? Would Parish be able to continue Ponthe's trip?

Yellow Feather and Lieutenant Cass approached as the sun set.

"Shall we bury him here, Parish?" Lieutenant Cass asked.

"Yes," Parish managed to say without rising.

The Shawnee men dug the grave on the high bank of the river. Yellow Feather and the boys gathered logs for the death house. Parish and Dasquorant carried Ponthe's body up the hill. They placed the body in a sitting position and built the small house-like structure over his grave. Parish and Dorothy took their places next to the grave. They wore their blankets over their heads, hiding their faces.

Lieutenant Cass and Yellow Feather brought them food.

Quitewe, the War Chief came once. "We will meet you at the Maumee Rapids."

"Yes," was all Parish succeeded in mouthing.

* * *

On the evening of the second day of mourning, Lieutenant Cass sat at the foot of the grave facing Dorothy and Parish. "Your father is no longer here, children."

Parish expected Dorothy to respond, but she maintained her silence.

"I wish I had memorized more verses," Lieutenant Cass said. "Or that we had kept the Bible. I found so much solace from its words."

The bereft couple remained silent as stones, as silent as Ponthe Walker, the father they both mourned.

Lieutenant Cass seemed driven to keep speaking to hammer through their catatonic state of grief. "When we were up north, around Mackinac and Sturgeon Bay, I found verses that explained the upheaval of the rocks and cliffs all around us. I memorized those that described the earth as a liquid."

The low tones of the Lieutenant's voice soothed Parish's nerves. Was Dorothy listening as intently? Parish needed to hear these words as much as the desert in his soul needed water.

"In Exodus 19:18 the Bible says, '...and the whole mount quaked greatly.' Deuteronomy 4:11, '...the mountain burned with fire.' In Judges, I forget the verse, '...The mountain melted from before.' First Kings 19:11, 'a strong wind rent the mount.' Job 28:9, 'he overturneth the mountains by the roots.' The Psalms tell us in 46:3, '...mountains shake with the swelling thereof;' in 104:6, '...the waters stood above the mountains;' and in 114:4, '...the mountains *skipped like rams.'* In Isaiah 34:3 the Lord tells us, *"...mountains shall be melted;'* Ezekiel 38:20, *'...the mountains shall be thrown down;'* Revelations 6:14, *'...every mountain and island were moved.'"* Lieutenant Cass stopped for a moment.

Neither Dorothy nor Parish responded.

"Ponthe was like a mountain to all of us, unshakable, unmovable, steady." Lieutenant Cass hung his head.

"But he's gone!" Parish's wail of anguish ripped through the air. He flung his blanket to the ground.

"I only know we are not to make our love of others replace our love of God," Lieutenant Cass said.

"I hate God," Parish spat the words.

Dorothy lifted her blanket. "You need to forgive God, Parish."

"No!" Parish's body felt like a stone. His mouth tasted like slate. He wanted to run, but there was no escape. "Do you have any more platitudes to add?" He glared at Lieutenant Cass.

"I know how you can feel peace, again." Lieutenant Cass spoke softly.

Parish had leaned forward to hear. The movement caused fresh awareness of grief's pain throughout his body. "Can you stop the pain?"

"The Lord can." Lieutenant Cass said. "Ask the Lord. John 3:16 says, 'For God so loved the world that he gave his only begotten son so that whosoever believeth on him should not perish but have everlasting life."

"I want to die," Parish said.

"Can you open your heart to accept the Savior's help?" Lieutenant Cass nearly whispered.

Parish heard the truth. His soul cried out for relief. "I wish I could."

A lark sang out to the receding day. Relief from travail hung like a promise within the bird's lonesome song.

Lieutenant Cass said, "Ask the Lord to be your Savior."

"God knows I need one." Parish looked at Dorothy, but her head was lowered under her mourning blanket. He was unable to follow any thought except to say aloud, "Lord, if you can help, please save my soul from all my confusion, vengeance, anger, hate, and self-pity."

Lieutenant Cass had taken Parish's hand. Its warmth or the setting sun spread a healing sense of comfort through Parish's body. His senses seemed to leave the boundaries of his pain-racked body, searching the entire ends of the earth to reap, to bring together every peaceful wind, scent, and lingering light.

Parish stood feeling renewed, at one with Ponthe's soul, as well as Dorothy's sadness. "My soul has been restored." He went to Dorothy and lifted her blanket. He knelt and embraced her as she sat on the ground. "We're going to be okay."

Dorothy looked at him, astonished. "You're okay, now." It wasn't a question.

Lieutenant Cass patted Parish's shoulder, stayed bowed and whispered, "Thank you, Jesus."

Chapter Twelve

On the third day after Ponthe's death, Parish collected the voyagers to leave the sad burial site on the bank of the Mississippi River. The clouds and storms that brought such havoc to St. Louis could have been a figment of Parish's imagination. Although he was refreshed by the Lord's hand, his grief lingered. He looked toward the heavens to search for any reason for continued concern, but the morning sky remained a bright blue.

Unasked, Yellow Feather, the whiteman adopted by the Shawnee, took Ponthe's place in the canoe with Parish and Dorothy.

Dasquorant preceded them, riding northeast on the shore of the Ohio River. Parish trusted they were heading toward the Wabash River. The Seneca's back was ramrod straight. His horse was a midnight-black Shawnee stallion named Thunder. Dorothy seemed to ignore the changing spring wonders of nature unfolding to concentrate on Dasquorant's progress.

Parish found no pleasure in his envy of the full-blooded native. He wished Beauty was with him to temper his emotions. His adopted mother would have brought his soul straight, in alignment with his best aspirations. Parish prayed, Please, Lord, don't let me stray from your path.

Parish knew he loved Dorothy, but his jealousy felt like hatred instead of devotion. Would Dorothy become the same sort of woman as his birth mother? Beauty told him his mother left her barren husband's bed to chase John Perry North, a romantic native-looking fellow.

Parish's white, birth-father's black dyed hair was originally the same color as the blonde ringlet his mother left for Parish North. What if he acknowledged he was entirely from a white bloodline, sporting the same hair color as both of their blasted blond heads?

All he had in his favor in Dorothy's eyes, would be the fact that he had been raised as a Huron hunter by Ponthe Walker and lived among Beauty's adopted Potowatomi tribe. But his white birth-father had been raised as a Potowatomi native, too.

Dasquorant was not white. The tall Seneca epitomized everything Dorothy wanted…to live in nature, without the constraints of a civilized white society.

Parish wondered where his soul had hidden the peacefulness he experienced on the day of his Savior's blessing. Why was he so far from God, now? Why was the devil, Dasquorant, tempting him by strutting that black fiend of a horse to attract Dorothy's affection? Suddenly, Parish felt as if the soul or the mind-set of Bishop Pascal had overtaken the treaty-voyagers.

"Please, Lord, have compassion on all of us." Parish hadn't meant to pray aloud.

But Yellow Feather and Dorothy both said, "Amen."

* * *

Two canoes pushed north up the Wabash River, against the spring thaws and fresh downpours. The current required more of a sustained effort than running with the flood down the Illinois River to St. Louis. Ponthe's absence was felt by every member of the orphaned treaty brigade.

For Dorothy, Dasquorant's constant image riding above them on the banks, or silhouetted against a high bluff or even a backdrop of green prairie grass, let her feel a larger hand, Ponthe's guidance, was present.

The dark side of Parish began to emerge with each day of added grief. His newfound confidence, after his conversion under Lieutenant Cass' guidance, seemed to dim his awareness of how he treated others. He compulsively complained at every infraction from Ponthe's routine. Nothing was left without a bitter comment directed to the sinner. It was almost as if evil stalked him, precisely because he now claimed to belong to the Lord. Dorothy didn't doubt Parish's intentions to turn his will over to his Savior. But she did wonder when she would determine the strength of his faith witnessed by his good works.

Henry Holt wasn't carrying enough supplies.

"Every man has to carry his own weight," Parish had barked, when they had camped at lunch.

"Sorry," Henry said. "I'll do better. I forget."

Jimmy Sweetwater needn't laugh at a jumping fish.

"You won't catch the stupid thing with laughter," Parish grumbled. "Use your net."

Dorothy wanted to cuff the back of Parish's head, but he was out of reach on the other side of the campfire. So she yelled, "Quit!"

Parish scowled at her over his shoulder. "Someone has to keep these people in line."

"Like your father did?" Dorothy shook her head. "You better keep the record straight. Ponthe never used a harsh word toward anyone."

Parish remained recalcitrant. "If you'd pay more attention to your supplies and cooking, I wouldn't be so grouchy from my growling stomach."

"What have I been paying attention to, if not to my job?" Dorothy took her time walking around the fire pit. She carefully laid her metal spatula on a level rock. She wanted to continue their argument unencumbered by a handy weapon.

Parish spread his stance as if prepared to fight. His face was distorted with hatred. "Keep your eyes off Dasquorant."

Dorothy was shocked. "Dasquorant?"

"He hasn't lifted a finger since we left the Mississippi." Parish smoothed down his beaded vest. "He eats our supplies and does nothing."

"I thought you asked him to find campsites for us," Dorothy said.

"I did," Parish admitted. "But he could take his turn at paddling."

Yellow Feather diligently minded the fire while the two of them squabbled. He bravely added a peace-making question, "Have you asked him?"

"No," Parish nearly shouted. "Who would ride his stupid horse?"

"I could," Jimmy Sweetwater called from the riverbank.

Obviously the entire conversation had traveled down to the shore.

Dorothy motioned for Yellow Feather to join Jimmy. Then, she pulled Parish's face close to hers, before quoting Blake, "I was angry with my foe: I told it not, and it did grow."

Parish leaned forward and kissed her forehead.

"That was Ponthe's favorite," Dorothy said, thankful for the kiss.

"I'll speak to Dasquorant when we camp." Parish sounded mollified. "I think I've been blaming him for Ponthe's death."

"Not more than he blames himself." Dorothy watched as Dasquorant rode down the bank toward them.

"He's also still a native," Parish said.

"And you're not?"

"Not anymore," Parish said. "Ponthe's dead and I'm white."

"Your mother...." Dorothy didn't know what she planned to say. That his mother lived as a native? But Beauty was probably half-white. One problem at a time. Peace with Dasquorant was more important. Where and how Parish and she decided to live in the future could wait.

"Beauty was white," Parish said. "She told me at Fort Dearborn. Renault gave her and her brother to the Potowatomi village. Renault dyed their hair black so they would be more readily adopted and accepted."

"I don't believe it." Dorothy said. "Beauty knows all the native ways."

"She does belong to the Midewiwins," Parish acknowledged. "But the Potowatomi taught my aunt everything she knows."

"Your aunt? You mean Beauty? Why did she tell you that story? Ponthe told you that your mother said your father was Potowatomi. Maybe Beauty's confused."

"Beauty is my aunt, Dorothy. The woman, my married mother, fell in love with a native. She deserted her husband and chased Beauty's brother, John Perry North. She wanted to live as a native! He was originally blond like me. Beauty says her hair is gray now, but she still dyes it black, as Renault did when he brought them, as youngsters, to the Potowatomi. Her hair was as yellow as the ringlet they kept from my mother."

Dorothy shook her head not in denial of Parish's words, but because she couldn't really decipher all the information.

Parish put both his hands on Dorothy's shoulders, as if she might flee.

"Renault didn't come across Ponthe by accident. He was following to find out where my mother settled. Beauty wanted to keep track of me." Parish voice dropped to a whisper. "My father was Beauty's brother, John. She told us her brother died of smallpox, when Renault was telling us about losing his family."

Dorothy found she was having trouble breathing. She tried to relax and took a deep breath. Was she afraid of Parish's passionate words? Was he telling her he didn't want her as his wife. Because he wasn't a native? Because she was white, too?

"Beauty made me promise not to let Ponthe know she had no native blood. Only Renault knows. Do you love me because I am living as a native, like my white father?

Suddenly everything made sense to Dorothy. "That's why you're jealous of Dasquorant?"

"Yes," Parish said, not letting go of her arms.

"I talked to Ponthe about our problem," Dorothy whispered, "not knowing how we would live after the trip…as whites or natives."

"Go on," Parish said. "What did he say, when was this?"

"I think it was on Sturgeon Bay." Dorothy tried to clear her mind of her own emotional turmoil. At least he still wanted to be with her. "No, no," she said. "It was after I nearly drowned and you hit me…to save me. You know after the Thames River, in the tent John Hicks gave me."

"That seems so long ago." Parish released her from his panicked grasp.

"Only earlier this year." Dorothy was amazed at how much had happened on the treaty voyage. The Bishop's suicide, the wedding they attended at Fort Mackinac, Ponthe's death. All the new people she had met.

"What did my father say?" Parish smoothed down his beaded vest.

Dorothy felt calmer, too, as she noted his habitual stalling technique. He was thinking with less emotion now, sorting out everything for them. "Ponthe said that Beauty and he would accept either decision." Dorothy leaned forward and kissed Parish's cheek. "Our life is up to us."

* * *

Dasquorant was a head taller than Parish, maybe two. Parish watched him tether the spirited black horse. He was startled, when the taller Dasquorant turned quickly toward him. "I've never ridden," he gulped.

"Not hard," Dasquorant said.

Parish handed a gift of tobacco to Dasquorant. "We have time for a smoke before the food is done."

Dasquorant nodded and followed Parish away from the others. "I want you to have the horse," Dasquorant said.

Parish appreciated the magnanimous give-away. "But I can't ride."

"Sell it," Dasquorant said. "Good horse."

"Fine horse," Parish said, offering the lit pipe to Dasquorant.

Dasquorant sucked in a mouthful of smoke, then blew it in the direction of the campsite, downwind. "Clan Mother will not believe I could kill Ponthe."

"Not you," Parish said to the Seneca's back.

"I caused it." Dasquorant turned his tormented face to Parish.

"Another man's hatred." Parish felt a wave of sympathy for the giant. "Ponthe knew you respected him. Bib Snake killed my father."

Dasquorant handed the pipe back. "And my hatred for Black Snake caused Ponthe's injury."

Parish took time to inhale, to think. "Why was there bad blood?"

"I won his horse with dice," Dasquorant explained. "I should have returned it. Ponthe would be alive."

"We cannot understand the ways of the Great Spirit." Parish wished Lieutenant Cass was with them to ease this man's pain. "Ponthe knows the truth of it, now."

Dasquorant nodded as if he too believed Ponthe had forgiven him, more than he forgave himself.

Parish honored the man's silence in remembrance of Ponthe Walker. His father was a quiet man, whose vision for natives in the white man's world included the harsh realities of power. Parish had been blessed to receive valuable guidance as a child. He trusted the Seneca Clan Mother had given Dasquorant all the wisdom she could impart. Parish wondered how he would guard his future children from the violence and cruelty in the world.

"Going up river against the spring tide will take us longer than walking," Dasquorant spoke softly.

Parish nodded. Amazed he was, at the change in tensions between them. Dorothy was right, confronting his own fears about Dasquorant solved half the issues.

"I worry Dorothy finds your native skills superior to mine."

"White woman only interested in your happiness," Dasquorant asked for the pipe. "I need to find a wife, too. Good cook."

Parish smiled at the compliment. "But the horse?"

"Let's portage for two days." Dasquorant handed the pipe back. "See how far we get."

"Good idea," Parish said.

"Teach you to ride," Dasquorant nearly smiled. Then a sadness made his shoulders slump. "Can never replace Ponthe."

"He's here," Parish said, sure of it.

* * *

Dorothy was proud of Parish. He had shucked off his meanness like a winter coat. Grief had blinded him to his own bitterness, for a time.

The sun shone for two days. The men walked with the canoes on their shoulders. Spring in southern Indiana Territory brought out the wild flowers and a range of returning song birds. The world celebrated more than spring. Perhaps peace would come to the region, and the settlers would let the natives farm their own fields. Maybe Ponthe was negotiating with the Lord to unburden the natives' lives. Dorothy hoped so.

Supper was rabbit stew and wilted dandelion greens fried with bacon.

Henry picked up a green piece. "What's this?"

"Good medicine." Dasquorant chewed on a big mouthful.

Jimmy Sweetwater stuffed his mouth in imitation. "Tastes like grass."

"Better than firewater for natives," Dasquorant said.

Jimmy stopped eating, rose and walked away.

"Is he native?" Lieutenant Cass asked Parish.

"Never occurred to me," Parish said.

Dorothy went to find the boy. He sat with his back to the white bark of a huge sycamore. Jimmy's knees were pulled up to an obviously aching stomach.

"I don't know who my parents were." Jimmy kept his head down. "People say because I like alcohol so much I must have Indian blood in me."

Dorothy sat next to the youngster. They were the same age, but he seemed so young. She handed him her piece of cornbread.

"Soon we will all be mixed up, Jimmy." She wanted to alleviate any worries for him. "If we haven't been raised native, or born native, we still have to learn how to live happily. I think America is going to become stronger and stronger. Each generation will get taller and braver from the combinations of races. You know when families marry cousins, babies get weak and die. So you see all this mixed blood can only make things better."

"I can't touch alcohol." Jimmy looked at her for the first time. "I know that much."

Dorothy rose and pulled the lad after her. "A lot of grown men and women haven't gained that much wisdom. You're going to have a fine life. Such a handsome lad." She rumpled his hair. "And, you're getting so tall, the ladies will be batting their eyelashes at you."

Jimmy seemed confused at that.

"To get your attention."

"Oh," he said, enlightened.

On the way back to camp, Dorothy was sure Jimmy had grown an inch, maybe two.

* * *

At Prophetstown, where the Wabash River heads east and the current was less rapid, the five men and one woman prepared to put their canoes back in the river. The Maumee Rapids would be reached by early June instead of late August. Ponthe had made good time in the early stages of the trip.

Parish consulted with Dorothy. "Are there enough supplies?"

"No coffee," she said. "And we need someone to hunt on shore, maybe meet us at the next camp site."

"Dasquorant can do it," Yellow Feather said, as he slid the canoe in the water. "He can ride fast enough to keep up with us."

"Is the horse really yours, Parish?" Dorothy asked.

"In theory," Parish said. "Too bad I can't ride very well. I don't think the horse likes me, either."

Dorothy laughed, then put her hand in front of her mouth. It was the first time she'd laughed since Ponthe had passed.

Parish hugged her. "Ponthe loved your laugh."

Lieutenant Cass came upon the weeping pair. "What happened?"

"I laughed," Dorothy said, then laughed again.

Parish joined her, tears running down his cheeks.

Lieutenant Cass laughed too, pointing at the discrepancy. "You're laughing with tears."

Chapter Thirteen

Fort Wayne

Fort Wayne was the first chance to replenish supplies for the troop since St. Louis. The Fort Commander granted access to all the provisions Lieutenant Cass requested. But Lieutenant Cass returned to the campsite with strange news. Natives were already gathering at Fort Meigs, only a day's travel to the east.

"The Chippewa," Parish said. "They're the last of the treaty tribes we were to contact."

"I only took a day's supply so we could travel faster," Lieutenant Cass said. "Was that a good idea? Why have they come so early?"

"Why should they plant crops they might not reap after they sign the treaty?" Parish understood the natives wanted to know which land they could sow to feed their families through the coming winter. "We will trade for supplies with the Chippewa." Parish put his arm around Dorothy's shoulder, to ease any worries she might have. "They're the richest tribe in the territory. Their commerce routes stretch all the way to the Grand Canyon."

"They have horses, too," Jimmy Sweetwater swatted Henry Holt's back, making the poor lad cough.

* * *

In the army tent they had carried all the way from the Thames River, Dorothy took off the buckskin dress Beauty had made with the pleated inserts. The cool spring night convinced to wear the lighter-weight traveling costume, the red spotted deerskin Parish had seen in his vision quest. Dorothy wrapped the pleated dress in the red gift blanket. She would see both prospective grandmothers in a surely less than a month; actually, Parish's aunt and her own dear mother. Dorothy rubbed her toughened hands over the package, remembering its giver. How would Beauty be able to bear losing Ponthe?

Dorothy laid out the form-fitting dress with its red circles of porcupine quills. According to Parish, Dorothy had promised generations to him in his vision quest. Maybe after the arduous trip came to an end and they were wed with her mother's blessing, she could finally be able to deliver on the promise.

Parish, Yellow Feather, and Dasquorant lingered at the campfire. Dorothy heard them rehearsing events for the treaty at Maumee Rapids. Ponthe would have let things fall together as they should. Unsure of their power, the young men tried to manage happenings in the future.

Dorothy wanted to stay awake to talk to Parish about where they would live after the treaty. She wasn't sure why Parish found it necessary to deny his native heritage. She was getting sleepy. She wrapped herself in a blanket and opened their tent door. "Parish," she called, twice. The other men laughed as Parish left the campfire to join her.

Parish took off his boots, preparing to get comfortable for their nightly talks.

Dorothy didn't really care what they talked about. She just loved having him all to herself, his low voice filling her ears with the music of their future life together. "I want to ask you about something."

"Ask and it's yours." As he sat down, he reached out and stroked her hair.

Dorothy forgot for a moment what all the urgency was about as she unbraided Parish's yellow hair. She combed his loosened hair with her fingertips. "I love your hair."

Parish put his arms around her waist. He kissed her mouth only for a moment then kissed her throat. "Love my white-man hair?" His hands moved to her waist. "Is that why you called me to your side?"

"Yes," she crooned. "I love to hear the sound of your voice."

"Most of the time, when I try to recall what we decided, I only remember your sweet caresses."

Dorothy pulled his head down to be kissed. "Where would Beauty like us to live?" She smiled, tangling her hands in his hair.

The tent was dark, and she couldn't see his face. Dorothy playfully rolled Parish on his back, really trying to remember what else she needed to talk about. Her body wouldn't let thoughts intrude on her brain when it was assaulted with so many pleasurable sensations. She'd remember her concerns for another day. She kissed him longingly, knowing that the time to have him all to herself was too short.

The next day after the portage from the Wabash River to the Maumee shore, Parish decided not to linger too long with Yellow Feather and Dasquorant after the evening meal. The walk had been easy and the dinner of rabbit delicious. Dorothy awaited his attentions. He got right to the point. "Dasquorant, you are a pure blood native. Yellow Feather, both your parents were white. My adopted mother, Beauty, is white. My adopted father was a native. I was raised a native, but my blood mother and father were white. I only know my father's name was North. How should I live to honor Ponthe Walker?"

"First, take the land allotted you at Maumee Rapids," Dasquorant said.

"Absolutely," Yellow Feather said. "Even I will receive a land grant as member of the Shawnee."

"But how should I live?" Parish asked again.

"What does Dorothy say?" Dasquorant busily packed his pipe.

"She says whatever will make me happy."

"But what will make her happy?" Yellow Feather stalled as Dasquorant lit the pipe, "There's your answer."

Parish stood. "I'll find out." He had to purposefully slow the pace of his short walk to Dorothy's tent. Lord, help me. Let me give You my life and my will. Create in me a new spirit and the strength to do Your will. Help me trust You more.

* * *

Fort Meigs

Twenty cone-shaped birchbark wigwams of the Chippewa lined the Maumee River bank at Fort Meigs. Dogs and children greeted the treaty crew as they helped to pull their canoes ashore.

"Horses." Jimmy shouted dragging Henry toward a corral.

Parish counted 30, maybe 40 animals milling about.

Okeinance sauntered up to Dasquorant, the tallest of their group. "I am called Young Chief."

Parish stepped forward. "I am Ponthe Walker's adopted son, Parish North. He died last month in St. Louis."

Young Chief put his hand on Parish's shoulder. "We heard of the tornado."

"Yes," Parish caught Dasquorant's eye. "A terrible accident."

"The gods are angry because we trade away Mother Earth," A young woman Dorothy's age spoke.

"My wife," Young Chief said. "Sheqinaik, or Black Bird."

"Ponthe's pick of sworn interpreters," Parish pointed to each of the crew. "Lieutenant C. Lewis Cass, Henry Holt, Jimmy Sweetwater, Dasquorant a Seneca, Yellow Feather of the Shawnee, and my intended wife, Dorothy Evans."

Young Chief inclined his body toward an old bent man, who winked at Dorothy. "Shinguax or Old Cedar." Then he named the men standing with him. "Wastuan, Penswegesic or Jay Bird, and our adopted white brother, Chemakeomon or American."

"Do you sell horses?" Jimmy couldn't help but ask.

"Trade," Black Bird said. "Or give-away."

The old man, Cedar, spoke, "We have one horse each for Ponthe's treaty travelers."

Henry and Jimmy let out loud yelps of happiness. They all followed the whooping boys to a muddied field enclosed with ropes. the carrel. Lieutenant Cass and Yellow Feather chose fine pinto mares. Dorothy excitedly chose a high-stepping roan beauty from among the many horses.

Parish declined the offer of another horse. "Dasquorant has given me his horse."

Old Cedar whispered behind his hand. "Give it back."

Dasquorant brought over a white, thick mare. "They call her Flicka. She's trained for children but won't let another horse pass her head."

Dasquorant's disappointment was evident. The horse he had generously given Parish, the black stallion, was prancing and neighing in the corral. Old Cedar gave Parish a knowing nod of his head.

"Dasquorant," Parish pleaded. "You know I can't ride the fine mount you gave me. Would you let me trade you for this more gentle one?"

It was the first smile Parish had ever seen on Dasquorant's face.

"Only if that is your wish." Without waiting for Parish to respond, Dasquorant let Flicka's lead fall to the ground. He strolled over to the corral and stroked Thunder's midnight blue mane. His urge to ride the quivering stallion got the better of him. Dasquorant suddenly jumped onto the fence and then slung himself onto

Thunder's bare back. He galloped down the flat river bank, away from the crowd.

Old Cedar still nodded his head. Parish wanted to hug the wise old man. He missed Ponthe's presence.

Parish didn't wait for Dasquorant to return from his ride. "I know the second article of the treaty by heart," Parish said to the group of natives. "The Chippewa will receive $1,000 each year for 15 years to be collected at Fort Detroit."

"They want our trade." Black Bird had turned to Dorothy.

Parish continued, "We expect 16 Chippewa will sign the treaty at the Maumee Rapids for their 640 acre tracts."

Young Chief and Old Cedar conferred.

"We intend to sign the treaty," Young Chief said.

* * *

Black Bird took Dorothy's hand. "Which tribe adopted you to replace a slain daughter?"

"I lived as a white woman at Fort Detroit," Dorothy said. "But I'm going to be married to Parish North."

"He said your name was Dorothy Evans." Black Bird wore her black hair loose except for a thin braid, which kept her luxurious tresses neatly tucked behind her ears.

Dorothy looked around the crowded campsite. "Where shall I set up a campfire to cook?"

"We cook from now on," Black Bird said. "The gods have been generous to the Chippewa. They watch our travels and rain riches on our heads."

An older woman came from behind one of the wigwams smiling. She held a coffee pot and six cups hung from a strap on her shoulder.

"It is a pleasure to be waited on," Dorothy said. "Your hair is so beautiful, Black Bird."

Black Bird laughed and circled her arm around Dorothy's waist.

"We have prepared a sweat lodge to inspire the treaty travelers for the Powwow." Old Cedar said. "Black Bird, will you find a sweat room for Parish North's woman?"

"I will, Father."

"I miss Ponthe." Dorothy started to sniffle. "He was my husband's adopted father, but I trusted him as mine, too. I never knew my father."

"Old Cedar will treat you as his daughter, now," Black Bird said. "Come this way."

* * *

Parish welcomed the luxury and the rigid discipline of the sweat lodge. The four-day fast would bring fresh dreams. His tears for Ponthe would be accepted as sweat. Henry Holt, Jimmy Sweetwater, and Lieutenant Cass had to be talked into the ordeal. "It's refreshing," Parish said. "Your mind and body will feel purified."

"I'd rather eat," Jimmy said.

"Me, too," Henry, Jimmy's shadow, said.

Lieutenant Cass seemed dubious, too. "Are we allowed to eat and leave the lodge when we wish?"

"Of course," Old Cedar said. "We offer the lodge as a gift not a prison."

The treaty travelers cheered up considerably. However, the heat put Jimmy and Henry immediately to sleep. American and Jay Bird dragged the boys out of the steamy room and let them sleep in a wigwam near the riverbank.

Lieutenant Cass gave it his best but succumbed to hunger when the smell of stew permeated the sweat lodge. He left with strong apologies.

Yellow Feather, Dasquorant, and Parish North benefited from the ordeal, as did Dorothy.

* * *

Parish dreamed his mother, Beauty, cried wrapped in his arms at the news of Ponthe's death. While Parish explained the circumstances, Ponthe appeared and touched his wife's face, comforting her. Parish felt strong. In his dreams, his role as lead interpreter at the Powwow pleased him. The white men bowed and scraped before him, asking his advice on every course of action. The natives met his every need with food and comfortable lodgings. Beauty was proud of him. Even Ponthe.

"No." Ponthe contradicted him in the dream. "You are the hands at the Powwow. Do for others. Humble yourself."

Parish understood the temptation of pride and rejected it.

* * *

In Dorothy's dreams in the sweat lodge, she played with babies. Lots of them. Almost too many to count. A great white house with too many doors kept the children busy running in and out. Just as

Dorothy completed a count of each and every one of the babies, toddlers, and children, more would dash out of the house.

"I can't have this many children," Dorothy told the people in the dream. "I'll never have time to get to know them."

"You will not see any of them in the summer." Elizabeth, her dream mother hinted at the answer to the riddle.

"Why not?" Dorothy was heartbroken. "Where do they go? Will they all die?" She woke up crying softly.

Black Bird was there with water. "Come outside. You are too close to your grief for Ponthe Walker."

"I think I was teaching school," Dorothy said. "I had lots of children around me and lots of books."

* * *

Yellow Feather would speak to no one after he came out of the sweat lodge.

"Leave his dream untouched." Old Cedar ordered. "No one is allowed to ask another of their dream's meanings."

Parish could tell by Yellow Feather's altered persona that no good would follow his white Shawnee friend. Instead of an open gaze and the trusting way he had previously carried himself, chest out, chin high, Yellow Feather's obvious fear made him seem furtive and stealthy. His eyes shifted from side to side, his shoulders were hunched as if expecting a blow, or worse.

When Dasquorant came out of the lodge, he kept asking, "Dorothy? Is she safe? Where is she?"

Parish immediately asked. "Why? Was she injured in your dream?"

Dasquorant uncharacteristically sat on the grass with his arms propped on his knees. He rubbed his eye with both hands, as if to wash away the pictures in his head. "I can't see her." Dasquorant nearly whispered to Parish, "Find her before it's too late."

Parish became alarmed as if catching the panic in Dasquorant's plea. He began to search everywhere, among the dwellings, behind the sweat lodges. He noted Dorothy's roan horse was still in the corral. He ran to the river only to find her peacefully napping on the grassy riverbank next to Black Bird.

The women looked like sisters. Their black damp hair from a recent swim after the sweat lodge ordeal, fanned out under their heads. Dorothy's skin was tanned as dark as Black Bird's. Their dresses were not dissimilar.

Parish decided if he wanted to live as a native, he wouldn't be able to fault the white skin of his wife. Her dark hair would let her pass. His yellow braids never would.

Chapter Fourteen

Maumee Rapids Powwow

Dorothy and Parish were reunited with the assembled firstpeople of the Old Northwest Territories. They remembered many of the natives they had met on the long trip around the Great Lakes. Their shared new worlds of people and places, joys, and sorrows were greater than either had anticipated when they originally began the journey at the Detroit River. Beauty and Renault shared their grief of losing their dear Ponthe. They sat with Dorothy and Parish late into the evening of the first day, reminiscing about the man and his contributions to peace.

"The Great White Father, President Monroe, sent Beauty his condolences." Renault sounded dutifully impressed.

"America has lost a great friend." Dorothy wondered if the Lord would ever replace such a soul. She watched the setting sun and realized, unlike tomorrow's daylight, the likes of Ponthe Walker would never return to earth. "We still need his guidance."

Beauty was no longer dying her gray hair. The white on the crown of her head and near her ears enhanced her beauty. The campfire brought a crystal radiance to her green eyes. "I wonder how my old husband explained his lack of faith to the Lord, once they met."

The four friends laughed softly, imagining the scene of integrity meeting ultimate goodness.

"No one could fare better," Parish said. "Renault, what do you think of my new name?"

"Sounds like a Catholic parish," Renault said. "Are you going to raise your children in the church?"

Parish shook his head. "Dorothy's ideas of religious freedom don't fit the concrete strictures of the Roman church. But I know the Lord does not find her wanting in any grace."

"Parish, you are turning into a great diplomat, like Ponthe," Beauty said. "I approve the transformation."

Dorothy smiled at their attention. "Old Cedar of the Chippewa has agreed to be my godfather. Renault, will you give me away at the wedding ceremony?"

Beauty and Renault exchanged glances. "Who told you?" Renault demanded.

Dorothy guessed immediately what he meant. "No one. But, are you telling me Father Sebastian and Mother are coming to the Powwow?"

"We expected them to arrive before you." Beauty laughed, then touched her throat. "I will never finish missing Ponthe." She took her son's hand. "Until I'm finally reunited in Orenda's world."

* * *

At the powwow grounds in the meadow below Fort Meigs, Parish had helped Yellow Feather secure their canoes. The number of natives seemed endless. Tents filled the tree-lined shore and the meadows beyond. Parish had hoped to have plenty of time to lay out locations for the different tribes to camp, before the powwow. After all, he'd arrived two months earlier than Ponthe had planned.

Yellow Feather still maintained his powerful sweat-lodge silence. His tense body reminded Parish of Jimmy Sweetwater's tight way of walking. His internal springs appeared tightened and Yellow Feather's fists were constantly clenched.

Parish did appreciate that the entire native population had honored their word to Ponthe to come to the powwow. They needed to find out where their government land allotments would be in order to start already-late spring plantings. His goal was to remain humble, in keeping with Ponthe's dream dictates, but he couldn't help smiling. He possessed all the information the natives needed.

After the second morning of greeting acquaintances and accepting condolences, Dorothy had begged to take a nap. Parish was too excited from all the attention to even sit down. How could he go off in the middle of the hot afternoon to take a nap? People would notice.

As he walked across the middle of the meadow surrounded on all sides by tents and teepees, Parish felt a surge of pride for his father. Ponthe had arranged all this. All these people counted on his adopted father to take care of them. Now they would count on him.

Parish squared his shoulders. Each step on the soft grass brought him nearer to the center of government activity. It was as if

Ponthe was sending the power of Mother Earth to reach him through the souls of his moccasins with her creative energy. Parish recognized he was up to the task at hand.

Then like a fist in his stomach, doubts arose. How could he, a white man, know what was best for these disinherited natives? He couldn't even decide where or how to live, when he married Dorothy. Lord, help me know Your will. He realized a sudden relief after giving his troubles to the Lord, who he trusted more and more.

The government agents he had met in Washington were gathered at the far end of the field. He wondered if they would even remember him, or his father. Parish recalled their names. The heat caused Bob Stukney, Stan Nigel, and Alan Forsythe to shed their black coats. They didn't dress or act like villains on a mission to cheat the natives. Parish thought he might not mind being counted among the ranks of the government's servants.

"How many sworn interpreters do we have for tomorrow?" Bob was a brusque speaking tall man with the makings of a light-colored mustache.

"At least two for each of the seven tribes," Parish said.

"If you'll take the Potawatomi," the oldest man, Stan Nigel, said. "That will leave us each with two tribes."

"You need to show them where to sign." Alan Forsythe loosened his collar button. "Spelling their names will be the hard part."

* * *

Dorothy tried to settle down for an afternoon nap on the second day of the Maumee Rapids powwow. Her mother's anticipated arrival was exciting, as was the prospect of the wedding. She would be all right once her eyelids could shut for a minute or two. The June sun was too hot. The emotional and pushing crowds hadn't helped conserve her energy. She let her mind linger on the events of the last two days.

The night before, Clan Mother and White Man had questioned Dasquorant in the presence of Beauty, Renault, Parish, and Dorothy. Parish repeatedly came to Dasquorant's defense, but Clan Mother wasn't appeased. "I will meditate about this," were the only words she would say.

Parish told Dorothy his own mother often used the same Midewiwin phrase. "They consult their familiars on the other side," he tried to explain.

Matthew and Thomas, Ponthe's Huron brothers, were more frail than she remembered. Their charming habit of finishing each others' sentences changed into a eerie watchfulness, as if each expected the other to suddenly disappear. Dorothy sympathized with them. Ponthe was no longer within their reach on this earth. They even walked differently, as if the fragilness of life could vanish under their next step. Both had aged dramatically in the few months since Dorothy had seen them together on the Thames River.

When she asked John Hicks if the men were all right, he told her the two were reconciled to Ponthe's passing. Dorothy didn't inquire how that was accomplished.

Ponthe did seem to be everywhere, near them. His name came readily to all the different tongues of the people gathered for the powwow.

Fort Mackinac has sent Supray and Antonette with letters from Mildred, Catherine, Charlotte and Mary asking for news. Ponthe Walker's death had been reported, but the Ottawa tribe was well represented.

The surly Delaware appeared as non-verbal attendees. Dorothy steered clear of the grumpy souls.

Brother Stiles from Fort Dearborn showed Dorothy his sketchbooks and language index system. He hoped to fill more books with gleanings from the different tribes at the powwow. "We're witnessing history," he told her.

Old Cedar, of the Chippewa, charmed the monk with his patience and introductions to his numerous relatives.

Today, Parish was off, fawning over the Indian agents from Washington. He was getting entirely too full of himself as far as Dorothy was concerned.

Dorothy's red-spotted dress hung on a hook just inside the tent, swaying to a cool breeze off the rapids. She could hear the crowds milling about. Voices rose and fell with the wind, reminding her of the sound of the lake surf before the Bishop got sick. Dorothy had intended to start reading, but she was so tired was asleep before the first page of Robinson Crusoe was finished.

The tent flap whipped open. Dorothy reluctantly got up to tie it closed.

Jimmy Sweetwater elbowed his way in.

Dorothy was nearly knocked over by the smell of whiskey. "Out," she shouted, pulling her blanket up from the ground.

"I thought you liked me." Jimmy knocked her to the floor as he fell on top of her.

She slapped his face. "Out you fool. Or I'll scream."

Jimmy's large paw covered her mouth. He'd grown stronger. Gotten heavier without her notice. "You're the only one who bats her eyelashes at me." Jimmy traced the curve of her eyebrow with his free hand. "How about a kiss?"

Jimmy released her mouth from under his hand.

Dorothy let out a scream. The loudest she could manage, considering the weight on her chest.

He hit her then.

"I need to see what...." The drunken mouth did not utter another syllable.

Dasquorant flung his half-nude body out of the tent.

Dorothy dressed quickly. Her mouth was bleeding. "Dasquorant," she called. "Bring him in the tent."

Jimmy had enough rope tied around him to keep a dozen men quiet.

"Gag his mouth," Dorothy said, as she tried to clean her face up.

Henry peaked in. "What's the ruckus?"

"Go get Parish." Dasquorant reached out and grabbed Henry's shirttail. "And my Clan Mother."

Dorothy was grateful for Dasquorant's steadying presence. Her split lip was beginning to swell. She felt confused, shamed and embarrassed at the same time. She sat down, wondering what Parish would do when he arrived.

* * *

Parish was pleased to help the government agents. "Most of the interpreters will know how to spell the tribal names."

"Could you list the interpreters for me?" Stan tapped the table. "Alan, write them down."

Parish wrote Henry Holt and Jimmy Sweetwater's names on the sheet of paper. "Here comes Henry now."

Parish laughed at the boy's antics.

Henry was running toward them. His hat blew off his head and he didn't stop to retrieve it. "Dorothy, Dorothy…." Henry looked longingly at a cup of water on the signing table.

"Help yourself," Stan said.

"Dorothy needs you," Henry managed. After gulping from the cup, he added, "Right away!"

"Tell her I'll be right there." Parish turned his back to Henry to sit down across the table from Alan. They needed to sort out the best interpreters for each tribe.

"Lad looked a bit upset," Bob said.

"Dorothy Evans has him wrapped around her finger." Parish smiled. "Me too."

"First for the Seneca from Point Pelee?" Alan asked, pen raised.

"Secoureweechta," Parish spelled the longer names out. "Also write down her white names: Whipping Stick or Clan Mother. And Wakenuceno, William Spicer or White Man, her young husband."

"Second, the Huron from the Thames River?"

"John Gurn or John Hicks and Matthew and Thomas Walker, the brothers of my father, Ponthe Walker."

"Sorry to hear of your father's accident," Stan said.

"Third, the Ottawa of Mackinac?" Alan was all business. No idle chatter escaped his lips.

"Supay and Walkeighke or McCarty."

"Fourth, the Delaware from Sturgeon Bay?"

Parish shivered from the memory of the cold stay, or something. He turned around, thinking he should have asked Henry what Dorothy wanted.

"The Delaware?" Alan repeated.

"Armstrong, the new chief, and Tahunquecoppi or Captain Pipe."

"Fifth," Alan droned on, "the Potawatomi. Sorry, Perish Walker."

"No," Parish said half-heartedly. "Hehawalk or Parish North." The native name Ponthe used when Parish was a boy called to him, lingered in his head. Parish could hear Ponthe's accent actually calling.

Parish looked behind him again. But he couldn't see Henry.

"We won't be much longer." Stan smiled. "Then you can chase after that woman of yours."

"Sixth, the Shawnee?"

"Othawakesek or Yellow Feather and Quitewe."

"And seventh, the Chippewa or Ojibway."

"Shinguax or Old Cedar and Chemakeonmon or American." Parish said.

"Could you ask them to come as early tomorrow morning as possible?" Bob pulled at the tight collar around his pudgy neck, then slickened his thin mustache.

"You can count on them to be here." Parish didn't plan to insult anyone by ordering them to report at dawn. The interpreters knew who they were, where they were needed.

Parish headed for Dorothy's tent. His thoughts returned to his family. Ponthe had been right: the government agents were only using him as a messenger boy. Did they think he was too native to join them? Somehow that pleased him, too native to join them, too white to....

Beauty, Renault, Clan Mother and Black Bird stood with grim faces on either side of the Dorothy's tent entrance.

Parish tried to embrace his mother. "Ponthe was right."

Beauty stepped back, avoiding contact.

"Where's Dorothy?" Parish asked, not waiting for an answer as he entered the tent.

Dasquorant sat next to a woman Parish could hardly recognize. One eye was nearly closed from the blow that had split her beautiful mouth. "Dorothy?"

She shook her head.

"What happened?" he asked Dasquorant ready to rip his head from his broad shoulders. Parish drew his knife. He felt like sliding it into his own chest but he brandished it at the large Seneca.

Dasquorant pointed to a roll of rope on the side of the tent opposite them.

Jimmy Sweetwater's eyes were closed.

"Drunk," Dasquorant said.

"He hit Dorothy?" Parish's mind slowed down to a worthless crawl. He felt as if all the air in his lungs had left him. He tried to breathe in but his stomach lurched.

Dasquorant rose to open the tent flap and left.

Beauty, Clan Mother and Black Bird crowded in.

Parish wanted to be alone with Dorothy. There was no room to breathe and his mind still refused to offer a complete thought. He dragged the bound Jimmy to the door. "Take him out."

The strong hands of Renault and Dasquorant pulled the inert Jimmy out of the tent in a second.

"Did he hurt you?" Parish asked.

Wrong, wrong question. Parish shook his head. One reasonable idea would help. Dorothy's faced was bruised past recognition. Parish's emotions threatened to choke him. He sheathed his useless knife.

"He didn't touch the rest of her body," Beauty said.

Dorothy nodded agreement. A single tear traced a slippery path down her swollen cheek. "I liked him," she croaked.

Black Bird brought her a cup of water. "Do you need to be in here?" she asked Parish.

"Yes," he said. "I'm late."

"Yes, you are," his own mother, aunt, glowered at him.

"Henry...." There was no excuse. Parish couldn't explain to the women gathered that he was about his father's business. He remembered the wedding ceremony story, when Jesus had told his mother similar words. But Parish should have returned as soon as Henry showed up. Ponthe Walker would have immediately known Dorothy would not have sent Henry on a trivial mission.

Would Dorothy hate him for not coming as soon as he was summoned? His morning's work at the treaty table hadn't amounted to anything of importance. Would Dorothy ever trust him again? He looked around the tent full of women to find a sympathetic face. None of the women smiled at him. Parish stumbled backward out of the tent. Lord, will Dorothy still marry me?

Lieutenant Cass caught his elbow. "I heard, Parish. Come sit down."

"How could God allow...." Parish couldn't continue the sentence. Nothing made any sense.

Lieutenant Cass spoke quietly. "Alcohol emboldens some."

"But Jimmy...was my friend." Parish felt like weeping. "Does she hate me for not coming as soon as she sent Henry?"

"Anger looks like hate." Lieutenant Cass wiped the perspiration from the rim of his officer's hat. "I'm sure her heart is big enough to forgive both Jimmy and you."

"Could you speak to her?"

"I'm not sure Clan Mother will let a man near Dorothy right now." Lieutenant Cass tore wide maple leaves from the tree they were sitting under. He placed the green leaves in his hat. "Keeps my head cooler," he explained.

Parish felt his own brains might boil in the hot passions under his skull. "What shall I do?"

"Best thing is to pray," Lieutenant Cass said, "when nothing else seems feasible."

Both men knelt under the tree. They closed their eyes and repeated the Lord's prayer together. When they were done, Clan Mother and Beauty were kneeling with them. Beauty nodded to Clan Mother, giving her preeminence in the discussion.

"Lieutenant Cass," Clan Mother asked. "Is Parish one of your believers?"

"He is a born-again Christian." Lieutenant Cass removed his hat. "Like me."

"Is Dorothy of the same faith?" Beauty asked.

Parish shook his head. "Dorothy admits to more doubts than faith."

Clan Mother stood. "Dorothy Evans is in a great deal of pain. Oh, not just her face. Her soul has taken blame for what has happened. Lieutenant Cass, are you able to restore her soul?"

"The Lord can."

"Parish," Beauty said. "Let Lieutenant Cass bring Dorothy the same peace you received after Ponthe's passing."

Lieutenant Cass stood and helped Clan Mother to her feet before offering his hand to Beauty. "With Parish's permission, I would like to help her."

Beauty put her hand on Parish's shoulder as he still knelt in supplication. "It's best."

"Will she ever be all right?" Parish asked. Nothing seemed more important. The treaty, the assembled natives, the opinion of the government's Indian agents, his own quandary of self-identification, all took a back seat to Dorothy's injury. Would she ever be able to forgive him for putting anything before her welfare?

Still on his knees, Parish humbly asked, "Can we find out who gave alcohol to Jimmy?"

* * *

Lieutenant Cass asked Black Bird to leave, but Dorothy clung to her dress. "Clan Mother and Beauty asked me to speak to you, Dorothy."

Black Bird unclasped Dorothy's fingers. "Clan Mother knows best."

Dorothy felt pulled into pieces. Where was Parish? She would rather have had Clan Mother sit with her than listen to Lieutenant Cass. What could he say to help? She really wanted her Mother! Dorothy didn't know if she was more angry or ashamed. She hung her head. "I told Jimmy women would bat their eyes at him."

Lieutenant Cass nodded. He fingered his hat nervously.

"Jimmy said I was the only one who flirted with him."

Lieutenant Cass shook his head. "Dorothy you must forget what he said. You are a friendly person looking after the younger lads."

"He's my age."

"Dorothy, you know he's not mature…and the alcohol."

"And Parish…."

"Disappointed you."

"Deserted me!" her whisper was harsh. "I hate him!"

"I know you are in pain. You were close by when I talked with Parish after Ponthe was killed." Lieutenant Cass seemed suddenly shy.

"Oh, you're going to solve everything with prayer, aren't you?" Dorothy looked around the tent to find something heavy or pointed to heave at the idiot. She could smell the heated canvas of the tent. From the feel of the swelling, she knew her face was hideous. Blood was still seeping down her throat. Dorothy felt she could rip the world apart if given half a chance. The very rocks would boil with one look from her.

"Not me," Lieutenant Cass said and looked at her with those honest gray eyes of his.

"Then what?" Exhausted from her spent anger, Dorothy began to weep.

"Are you in pain," he asked quietly.

"No." She wanted to scream but she was just too tired. "I'm furious!"

"The Lord will relieve all your anger."

"I don't want to be forgiven." Dorothy felt like a lost child. "I want Mother, here."

Lieutenant Cass nodded his head. "May I pray aloud?"

Dorothy didn't know if she'd given him permission or not, but he began a long prayer.

Make me a channel of your peace, Lord. Where there is hatred, let me bring seeds of love; where there is wrong, let me bring the spirit of forgiveness; where there is discord, let me bring harmony, where there is darkness, let me bring light; where there is doubt let me bring faith; where there is despair, let me bring hope; where there is sadness and fear, let me bring joy and trust; where there is error, let me bring truth. Lord, grant that I may comfort rather than to be comforted, understand rather than to be understood, to love rather than to be loved. For it is by self forgetting that one finds, by forgiving that one is forgiven and by dying that one awakens to eternal life.

"You believe the Lord saved you?" Dorothy could feel her body relaxing.

"He promised," Lieutenant Cass said.

"If I could pay for the peace of mind you seem to have, I would..." Dorothy sighed, "gladly."

"I know it's grandiose of me," Lieutenant Cass hung his head. "But I want a God I can love, so sometimes I forgive God."

"I've done that," Dorothy said.

"Then you want to be a Christian?"

"I want what you have." Dorothy was amazed at her sudden desire to finally be reconciled to the Lord. "Is it peace of mind?"

"The Lord's spirit will fill you with peace."

Dorothy reached out her hand. All the blood hadn't yet been washed off.

Lieutenant Cass didn't hesitate to grasp Dorothy's hand. Lord, accept Dorothy you're your fold. Her heart is open and she accepts you as her Savior." Lieutenant Cass tilted his head. He expected a response from her.

Agreeing to all the vows in the world, Dorothy said the words she would say at her wedding, "I do."

The darkness in the shaded tent took on a purple glow. The sun had found some piece of radiance outside to change the heated atmosphere. Dorothy heard a ringing in her ears and then the sounds of the birds outside. Her mouth had stopped bleeding. The pain inside her skin, inside her heart and head were gone.

"It's real," she said.

Lieutenant Cass smiled. "I know."

He left her then, but the women quickly re-entered the tent.

Dorothy couldn't smile, but she thought the women knew she had changed. She was no longer injured, no longer shamed.

Clan Mother spoke. "We should leave Parish and Dorothy to sort this out."

Parish slowly entered the tent, as if he was reluctant to face her anger. He swallowed and finally repeated over and over, "Forgive me, forgive me" as he knelt beside her, lowered his head into her lap.

"I'm one with you, now." Dorothy cradled his head.

"You've accepted the Lord, too?"

"Thank God," they said together.

* * *

Later in the evening, when Dasquorant brought Parish the battered body of Yellow Feather, Parish knew why Yellow Feather had decided never to speak again after his sweat-lodge dream. His white friend was still breathing, but his body was badly beaten.

Beauty helped Parish set the broken bones in Yellow Feather's right arm before he regained consciousness.

"He'll probably lose use of the arm," Beauty said.

Clan Mother brought Henry Holt and Dasquorant to the tent.

Crowds of natives formed a semi-circle around the campsite. Clan Mother had the ear of Henry firmly in her grasp. Dasquorant followed even though he was too tall for her to reach his ear.

"Tell them what happened," Clan Mother commanded.

Parish cringed to realize he'd brought so much violence to the peaceful powwow. Ponthe would have pulled his ears for years over this debacle...if he'd been alive.

Dasquorant seemed befuddled and began to tell the crowd how Ponthe had been killed. "An accident meant for me."

As Dorothy came out of the tent, she pulled the hood of her dress over her head to hide her bruises. The crowd had taken in a collective breath at the sight of her painful, disfiguring injuries.

Dasquorant seemed in a daze, or drunk himself. "Shenenstu or Big Snake was about to tip a heavy beam onto my head, when Ponthe Walker pushed me aside. He died. We buried him beside the Mississippi."

Matthew and Thomas, Ponthe's brothers stood side-by-side, next to Beauty. Renault was behind her.

Matthew spoke. "Ponthe said he would make a gift to the Great Spirit for the Hurons at the great Mississippi River. I don't think he knew it would be his own life."

"He gave up his life for his brother," Clan Mother said.

"No greater gift," Parish said, taking Dasquorant's hand.

Beauty went to Dorothy and put her arms around her.

In the ensuing quiet, Henry stood as if he'd found the courage to speak. "Yellow Feather was given the liquor by that Shawnee, Big Snake. Black Hook and Wolf were threatening to take Yellow Feather's horse. He didn't want to trade, so after they beat him, they forced the alcohol down his throat and left him with the bottle. Jimmy picked the bottle up and drink it all down."

Dasquorant stood, too. "I must give the black horse to Big Snake. I won Thunder from him in a dice game. All this bloodshed is on my head."

Parish patted Dasquorant's shoulder, leaving his hand on it. "The white men have told you since you were born that nothing you could do could wipe away the fact that you were native. Your native generosity has not caused any harm to any one."

Clan Mother pushed Parish's hand aside. "Give the evil horse back."

"I will, Clan Mother." Dasquorant said.

The appeased crowd dispersed.

Chapter Fifteen

Dorothy tried to comfort Parish, but her face felt ripped open. Even more pain had to be endured when Beauty insisted on sewing up her lip with needle and thread. Parish went outside, and Dorothy could hear him retching.

Renault brought her a bottle of rum to ease the pain. But, the open cut hurt even more from the disinfectant. He patted her back. "Sorry, little one. It had to be done."

The next morning, the swelling seemed even worse.

Parish was no help. "It's green now," he said, bringing the sound of his words up at the end of the sentence to make it sound like a happy event.

Black Bird was a wiser friend. She offered oil from a leaf that looked like part of a cactus. "From the desert," she said. "No scar will remain."

Parish pained Dorothy as much as her face. He wouldn't leave the tent. The treaty organizers needed him. They kept sending different interpreters for him, as if he had misunderstood the original messengers.

She'd had just about enough of Parish's sulking silence.

"Come with me." Dorothy lowered her hood over her forehead and tied a silk sash from Black Bird around the lower half of her face.

Out in the field surrounded by campsites, men and women were lined up in four rows to sign their names to the treaty. The bright blue sky made the water sparkle as the river meandered over the mud flats. Cottonwood dotted the branches among the just greening willows along the bank. Dorothy smiled at the grandeur of the Lord, even though the stitches pulled painfully. Why couldn't Parish shake off his despairing mood?

"Get in line," she told Parish.

"I'm supposed to be at the table," he said.

Beauty came up behind them. "Get up there before I drag you myself."

Parish walked toward the table.

As far as Dorothy could tell, he slumped his way there. "What's wrong with him?" The two women said in unison and then turned to each other and laughed.

* * *

Parish looked back at the two women in his life. Their derision weighed him down even further. His place at the end of the treaty table was being manned by Lieutenant Cass.

"Should I interpret for you?" Parish asked.

"No, no." Lieutenant Cass stood up. "Sit. You look like you need a chair. I could take Henry's place as interpreter. I left Jimmy in the stockade's lockup."

Parish followed Lieutenant Cass's gaze as he pointed up the embankment to Fort Meigs' formidable log walls. Threatening iron cannons were still aimed at the position of the British's old 1812 Maumee River attack. Instead of uniformed soldiers, the powwow meadow between Fort Meigs and the river was packed with natives seeking peace and property. Their campsites filled every available space on the flat of land.

Parish handed a freshly dipped pen to the next native in the line before him. Captain Lewis, a Shawnee, took the pen. Parish looked down the table.

Alan the youngest member of the agency, was seated next to him. Alan's printed sign which lay on the table read, "Seneca and Huron."

Parish called to the oldest agent at the far end of the table, "Stan, I can't see who you are signing up."

"Ottawa and Delaware."

Parish turned back to send Captain Lewis to Bob Stuckey's Shawnee and Chippewa line, but Captain Lewis was nowhere in sight. The pen was back on the table. "Where did he go?" he asked Lieutenant Cass.

"Don't know," Lieutenant Cass said. "Must have realized his error.

Parish began to pay attention to the signings. The Potawatomi were supposed to total 31 signers. "How many signatures have you received?"

Lieutenant Cass started to count the x's and spelled scrawls. "Fifteen."

"There are more than 16 in the line in front of me." Parish counted heads again to make sure. He remembered the number in Article Two. "The Potawatomi are only scheduled for 31 to sign the treaty."

The Trout, Wynemakowo, asked. "Where do I sign?"

"Right here," Parish said. "Lieutenant Cass, read off those names to me."

'They're mostly 'X's."

Parish tried to forget his suspicions. Maybe his own disgrace with Dorothy made him look for the errors of others. His head hurt from the sun, or something.

"Count," Ponthe ordered from somewhere in Parish's head.

Lieutenant Cass started reading names, "Chechalk, Wynemakowo, Hiawichemon...."

Parish handed the pen to the next Potawatomi in line, Wawcacee.

Flat Belly was next in line. "Sorry to hear about the attack on Dorothy," he said. "Mrs. Evans and Father Sebastian were packed and set to leave before I left the fort. They should be here soon."

Parish bowed his head, concentrating more on the list Lieutenant Cass was reading. "White Elk, Saguemari, Missensusai, Papikitcha, Waninsheway."

"Stop," Parish said. He pulled Lieutenant Cass down to his ear. "Cross one of those out. That's White Elk."

Lieutenant Cass whispered back, "They're signing twice?"

Parish nodded. "To get more land."

"What's going on?" Bob called.

"Another message from his wife," Musket, the next in line, said and winked as he took the pen and signed another 'x'.

Parish dotted the mark with a huge drop of ink, obliterating it completely.

"We'll get it figured out," Lieutenant Cass said. "I made a mistake."

"Better not," Stan called. "President Monroe's henchmen will be happy to throw the whole treaty out if there is any infraction of procedure found."

Crane signed an 'x' which Parish promptly crossed out; since Crane had already signed as Chechalk.

Parish said under his breath to Lieutenant Cass, "We may have to throw out all the x's."

Lieutenant Cass continued to read, "The Trout."

Parish crossed it out.

Lieutenant Cass tried again, "Corn."

Medouin or Corn stood in front of Parish reaching for the pen.

"Corn," Parish said, refusing to give him the pen. "You're in the wrong line." Parish wondered if he could handle the situation. Please, Lord, help me.

Five Ottawa natives dropped out of the Potowatomi line in front of Parish.

The Godfrey brothers signed their names, as did Beauty. Seventeen villagers from the Raisin River signed more 'x's'. Parish signed his name, the 31st and last. He thought about the deceit of the natives. Maybe because they realized Lieutenant Cass would not catch their deception, they couldn't resist the temptation to take as much land back from the whites as they could. He was as guilty as any of them, since he knew both his mother and father were whites who had been adopted into the Potowatomi tribe. His own adoption by Beauty was the sole technicality allowing him to claim land.

"We're done," Parish said to Stan. "We have all thirty-one signatures."

"Could you stay here and help with the Seneca?" Alan asked. "I'll be right back."

"The total Seneca is supposed to add up to 83," Parish said.

As soon as Alan left and Parish and Lieutenant Cass took over, the line in front of the table got a lot shorter.

"What's going on," Stan called again.

"Wrong line," Lieutenant Cass answered again. "Parish has it under control."

Parish didn't know if a deception occurred or Clan Mother had just misunderstood. She had signed three times, once for each name. Parish didn't even ask. He crossed out Clan Mother and Whipping Stick, making a note next to each, "Wrong Line."

"Count the names we have," Parish instructed.

"Forty-nine," Lieutenant Cass said softly, "and sixty x's."

Captain Signore stood in front of Parish. He signed Samendue. Skilleway signed Robin, Jo signed Aquasheno, Big Turtle signed Skekoghkela, and Civil John signed Methomea.

William Spicer and Dasquorant were the last in line. "We gave them the message," Spicer said.

"Good," Parish said, "Now go to the end of those two lines and pass the message along. Ponthe knew how many in each tribe should sign. We're throwing out 19 extra x's for the Seneca."

Magically, the lines in front of Stan Nigel and Bob Stukney melted away.

* * *

A week after the Washington Indian agents had left with their signed treaty, the government tables were used for the powwow's mountains of food. Parish was astounded at the variety.

Beauty came up behind Parish and tapped his back, just as he was about to reach for a piece of flattened bread. She informed him that Father Sebastian and Dorothy's mother had arrived safely and were housed at Fort Meigs. "Elizabeth has three trunks filled, not only with wedding clothes for you and Dorothy, but also with sweets, breads and dried fruits for the banquet."

"So she approves of our marriage?" Parish had replaced the bread.

Beauty surprised him. "You may not recognize Father Sebastian."

"Has he been ill?"

"No." Beauty smoothed down her whitening hair. "He has changed, considerably."

Parish remembered how aged Ponthe became on the trip. "Tell me."

"Dorothy's mother missed her terribly," Beauty said. "Father Sebastian and Elizabeth comforted each other."

"Of course," Parish said. "They would."

"So Father Sebastian has left the priesthood and married Dorothy's mother." Beauty finished her explanation just as Elizabeth Evans and a man in a frock coat approached.

"Thank you for preparing me," Parish said quietly to his mother.

Father Sebastian embraced Parish. "Thank God, you are safe."

"And you," Parish said, accepting a hug from Dorothy's mother as well. "I've heard your news."

"Will Dorothy understand?" Elizabeth asked as Father Sebastian slid his arm around her waist.

- 166 -

Parish understood his answer was crucial to their happiness. "She loves you both," he said, happy to find a diplomatic way to answer.

Elizabeth excused them. "Sebastian, could you let Beauty and Parish show you the camp sites? I need to speak to my daughter."

Without waiting for them to reply, Elizabeth entered Dorothy's tent. Parish heard Dorothy's exclamation of joy.

* * *

After Dorothy had wrung all the love she could out of her mother, she invited Elizabeth to sit down for a long overdue conversation.

"I want to hear everything about your recovery from the attack." Elizabeth reclined with an elbow propped on one of their bedrolls. "Beauty says you've become a Protestant."

"I don't think so," Dorothy said.

"Lieutenant Cass converted you?" Elizabeth tried to make herself more comfortable.

"Well, yes." Dorothy worried the scarf she still wore around her neck. She sat down next to her mother. "After Jimmy hit me, I was ready to kill poor Parish."

"What stopped you?" Her mother tenderly undid the red scarf and cradled Dorothy's chin in her hand. "Parish was supposed to protect you."

"He was busy with the treaty." Dorothy could see her mother would need time to weigh what had happened. "When Jimmy came after me, I was alone here."

"Beauty says you forgave Parish?"

"And Jimmy; but not until Lieutenant Cass helped me pray." Dorothy looked around the tent. The purple glow that had filled the air wasn't visible now. "Something more than being able to forgive Parish happened. Something more than me helped me. I'm no longer a doubter."

"So," Elizabeth said. "because your prayer was answered, you're not going to go to mass anymore?"

"I don't know about that." Dorothy said. "I might need to talk to Father Sebastian. But it seems to me if Jesus died once for all our sins, we should accept him as our Savior. Then the liturgy of the mass need only be attended as a thankful remembrance."

"But that is what the mass is," Elizabeth said.

Dorothy nodded. "Do you approve of Parish?"

"Of course," Elizabeth said.

"And Father Sebastian will marry us?"

"If he doesn't, he'll never eat another morsel of my cooking." Elizabeth laughed and then explained how her own new marital status had come about.

* * *

Father Sebastian had also brought along a young boy of thirteen, named Silas Douglas. "Silas is not a Catholic," he explained to the family gathered outside Dorothy's tent, "but he attends mass at Fort Detroit. Silas is interested in everything and asked to come along."

Silas spoke for himself, "I met Brother Stiles from Fort Dearborn today. He tells me I may be witnessing history. This could be the last treaty re-distribution of Indian lands in my generation."

Henry Holt caught Silas' introduction, too. "A friend of mine, Jimmy, can't exercise the Chippewa pony Old Cedar gave him. Would you like to go for a ride?"

Silas disappeared quickly with Henry.

"How much longer will Jimmy need to stay in prison," Dorothy asked.

Parish answered, "Lieutenant Cass says a year will help clear his brain of the alcohol."

* * *

In the middle of the meadow, Clan Mother, Beauty, Black Bird, Dorothy and Elizabeth cut away a six-foot square of turf. Dasquorant and Parish lifted the sod carefully to one side, to be replaced after the dance. Eagle feathers were laid on lines drawn lovingly into Mother Earth.

Drummers, flute players, rattle and whistle experts gathered on the west side of the field.

Dorothy hardly recognized Clan Mother when Black Bird got through with her Earth Mother costume. They both wore small buffalo headdresses and their faces were painted yellow. In the Pueblo fashion that the Ojibway had brought to the powwow, each wore a dark woven dress covering her left shoulder and leaving the right arm bare. Clan Mother's long gray hair was worn loose, hanging down her back. It contrasted with Black Bird's blue-black locks. Dangling from their right elbows, bunches of orange feathers fluttered. Large turquoise beads hung around their necks and turquoise-colored sashes wound around their waists. Their white skirts were bordered in blue, black and red. Every move that Black Bird made, Clan Mother mimicked, unlike the unique male dancers' steps.

Parish told her the song was one of rejoicing at the coming summer and the dawn of wisdom.

The singers intoned, "Grandfather, Ponthe, has given us a sacred path."

The dancers all wore wreaths of sage around their heads.

Parish danced with the others, but Dorothy's face was too painful for her to join in. She remembered the dance of the Ottawa in the snow when Charlotte married Philip Raven, as well as the Dream Dance at Fort Dearborn when she fainted from the mesmerizing music. His walk across the meadow to the treaty table had been a beaten man's. Now, his Earth Mother dance steps held all the pride Dorothy had seen in him before she'd been brutalized by Jimmy.

Lieutenant Cass wasn't dancing. It was good of him to keep an eye on the casualties of the treaty trip company. Jimmy Sweetwater was furloughed for the celebration. Yellow Feather was comparing his injuries with the younger man's. Both had been adopted by the Clan Mother, after they'd pledged never to touch alcohol. Their allotments of land would come in handy for the farming Seneca tribe. She also recognized Clan Mother's power over Jimmy's drinking, as well as her need to provide Yellow Feather company. Also, William Spicer's trading post would need employees.

"What has restored Parish?" Dorothy asked Clan Mother, when she had ceased her part of the dance. "After Jimmy attacked me, he seemed more broken than I was."

"After Yellow Feather was tortured," Clan Mother told Elizabeth. "Parish felt defeated."

"You're right." Dorothy was fascinated by Parish's freedom from any sort of self-censure in his dance.

Dasquorant had tired from the dance. He busied himself with courting Black Bird's younger sister. Parish danced on and on, with no lessening of energy.

"If anything built him back up," Lieutenant Cass said. "It was his resolve to keep the treaty's integrity."

"How did he manage that?" Elizabeth asked.

"He didn't let anyone sign twice for land." Lieutenant Cass said.

"I understand, now," Dorothy said. "Ponthe's spirit dances with him."

* * *

Parish joined the group surrounding Dorothy.

Her mother smiled at him. "Have you asked my daughter to marry you?"

"Not officially." Parish knelt before Dorothy in full view of the powwow. "Will you let me care for you, father the children you want to bring into this world? Will you allow me to give you all the affection I possess?"

"I will." Dorothy pulled him up to her and flung her arms around him.

"I now pronounce you man and wife," Father Sebastian said.

"Will that be enough of a ceremony?" Elizabeth asked.

"Why not?" Beauty asked.

"Their hearts are already one." Renault held out a gold wedding ring. "This was my wife's mother. Our daughter was still alive when my wife insisted I keep it."

Parish slipped the ring onto Dorothy's finger. "With this circle of love, I promise to be at your side for the rest of our lives together."

Sebastian blessed the newlyweds. May the Lord bless you and keep you. Shine his light into your hearts and constantly receive your prayers.

"What about the wedding dress I made?" Elizabeth asked.

"I'll wear the dress at the reception in Fort Detroit," Dorothy said.

"After a long camping honeymoon." Parish hadn't let go of his bride.

* * *

Finally, alone in their marriage tent, Dorothy's hands spread Parish's long yellow hair over their shoulders, luxuriating in its abundance. When Dorothy rolled on top of Parish and bent to kiss him, the soft folds of her dark hair fell loosely over her shoulders onto his face.

In the soft twilight, he could see her enjoying each sensation. "My woman." He nestled his head in her neck. "Our love will only get better."

Dorothy pulled both his ears. With his face close to hers, she said, "Remember that part of wedding vows about leaving your mother and father and cleaving only unto me?" She let go of his ears and kissed him. "This secret, the way we give pleasure to each other, will help us remain faithful to each other."

Perish said, "Renault will think I've become a man."

Dorothy tilted her head to question that.

"By not bragging," he said, kissing the palm of her hand before tracing a line with his tongue from her palm to her wrist.

Chapter Sixteen

Fort Detroit, Fall 1818

A year older than when she had left Fort Detroit, Mrs. Parish North and her husband, Parish, re-entered the gates of Fort Detroit. Lieutenant Cass had returned to Washington with the Indian Agents to hand President Monroe the signed treaty for the Erie Canal's peaceful construction. Only Black Bird's father, Old Cedar, remained at the fort.

Before Dorothy and Parish left for their honeymoon campout, Black Bird had confided her fears of the future. She pleaded with Parish and Dorothy to send Old Cedar to Fort Detroit with Dorothy's mother and Father Sebastian. Under their protection as whites in a white world, Black Bird hoped her father would see a more comfortable old age. The Chippewa could only offer the old man years of traveling along their rigorous trade routes.

Black Bird had explained, "I want his old age to be blessed with ease."

With the passing of Ponthe Walker, both Dorothy and Parish felt they needed the wisdom of an older man. "Thank you for your great gift," Parish had said.

They both wept when they encountered Old Cedar just inside Fort Detroit's gate. He had opened his arms for them both. Dorothy welcomed her new father into her heart, too.

Dorothy noted the late hour of morning meant her mother would be finished with the breakfast chores. Of course, Elizabeth would be eating with her husband, Father Sebastian, now. Dorothy wondered if Beauty had ever told Elizabeth that she had predicted twins for grandchildren.

The courtyard of the fort sported the same dogs and lazy soldiers, loitering or trying to look busy at some repetitive, useless task. Dorothy shook herself remembering how she had considered cooking an unending, meaningless chore until the treaty trip. Now, she felt proud to have kept the bodies, if not the souls, of the treaty crew ready for each day. Even though she no longer felt demeaned as a cook, she still wanted more out of life.

Dorothy wanted her teeth in a book.

More than her husband's tug on her heartstrings, more than the longed for companionship of her mother, Dorothy wanted to see the Jesuit library. If it was still intact, unsullied by the Bishop, undamaged by the winter winds. She wanted to know if her mind had remained unscarred by Jimmy's foolishness. If she could stand in the library all would be harmonious in an unsure world. The rows of books mattered. They held together the histories of people and promised security in the future.

"Dorothy," her mother's voice weakened her knees.

They embraced inside the door of the rectory. Dorothy remembered her smell, the feel of comfort from her soft round shape, her soft hair and whisper of a kiss. "Oh, I missed you. Where have you been?"

"Right here, silly." Her mother wiped away the tears on Dorothy's face. "You're the one marching off to trap a husband." She patted Dorothy's stomach. "Are the twins expected yet?"

"Beauty did tell you?"

Parish started to speak, but Elizabeth hugged him into silence. "Parish. Plenty of time for babies. The Raisin River needs a town name to label all those buildings." Elizabeth held her hand over her mouth for a second. "You'll see soon enough."

Father Sebastian shyly hung behind Dorothy's mother. "Mr. and Mrs. North. Dorothy, your mother has missed you both. We almost couldn't talk her into cooking for us."

Elizabeth swiped at the ex-priest with her apron. "Don't be telling tales out of school. I knew you were safe with Ponthe Walker."

She took Parish's hand. "A fine man, your father was."

"Come in, come in," Father Sebastian held the door to the rectory open. "We'll have a cup of coffee and you can tell us all about the adventures on your long honeymoon."

Parish pulled Old Cedar into the rectory. "The Chippewa have given us a great gift of wisdom. Thank you for caring for our friend, Old Cedar, while we were gone."

Father Sebastian and Elizabeth both bowed to the elder, who seemed right at home in his honored position in the family. Old Cedar touched Elizabeth's face. "What a pleasure old age is, when our youngsters listen to us."

"Bishop Pascal...." Dorothy started, trying to remember the confession she had memorized something about unknowingly ruining the prelate's life.

"Needn't be mentioned, again." Father Sebastian lifted his hand as if to erase the Bishop's memory. "God will judge who He will."

Parish spoke her mind. "I think Dorothy would like a moment to herself in the library."

They let Dorothy pass them, her mother was wiping away her own tears now. Father Sebastian opened the library door. Dorothy looked back once at Parish, as if apologizing for her lust for the printed page.

"We'll be here," he said without a hint of censure, as he shut the door behind her.

And she was alone with the tomes. She ran her fingertips over the lower books. The ones she'd read and tried to read. The collections by authors she'd tasted but not digested and the duplicates Father Sebastian had encouraged her to underline, if she felt the need. They all stood ramrod straight at their appointed stations.

She opened Sir Walter Scott's Waverly. At random, she read the phonetically spelled dialogue of a Scottish peasant. Dorothy let it lay on the couch and reached for the Bible. The 70th Psalm of five verses opened. She read the last verse, the one with the word 'tarrying,' where an arrogant David pleaded with God not to be slow in his aid. She spun around in the center of the room.

Here was her reality, locked in safe covers, patiently awaiting her return...unchanged.

However, civilization had not provided the sublime pleasures and beauty she had discovered in nature. Canoeing on three of the four Great Lakes let her feast her eyes on the sparkle and sheen of their iridescence. The books around her captured ideas, but nature provided all of God's glory. Her adolescent moods were often quieted among those very words. Her passion for adventure appreciated the new horizons she'd experienced to satisfy a greater need. The titanic forces evident in the marvels along the coastlines as well as the inspiring and peaceful meadows and glades under natural oak openings silenced any restlessness.

In the pure air, in the paradise of nature, Dorothy thanked the Lord she was able in her time of need to be guided to a closer understanding of His love and reconciliation with the people He created. She trusted when she was bereaved in the future or disappointed in the actions of others her personal Savior would let her cling closer to His heart.

Would she have come across the Lord's love among the precious books on the library shelves surrounding her? Perhaps she needed the awe and respect for nature as a first step toward realizing the Lord was actually interested in her. He witnessed when the wren fell from the sky and He dressed the fields in His radiant splendor. Surely humans never lost His attention moment by moment.

Dorothy thanked the Lord for His blessings. She no longer needed to tarry here, searching for more information, more answers. Life awaited the mature woman she'd become.

* * *

After the reception, where they had dressed in whitemen's wedding finery, Parish and Dorothy enjoyed one night of married life in the canopied bed of the rectory's guest room. The next morning they said their farewells and walked overland to the Raisin River.

Old Cedar had wanted to stay at Fort Detroit, near Elizabeth. "Not just for her cooking." He'd winked at Dorothy.

The sun was setting as they reached the river. It glowed a ruddy color from the sun or scarlet maples along the shore. Parish looked up to his favorite hill of oaks and was shocked to see a white mansion set among the ancient trees.

"Whose house is that?" Dorothy asked.

"I don't know," he said. "It wasn't built a year ago."

"Where is your mother's wigwam?"

"A few more yards downstream," he said. As he rounded the shoreline, expecting to see the smoke from his mother's native home, he was met with an empty field of grass. Across the river, he was relieved to see the Potawatomi village intact.

"Where is it?" he asked Dorothy.

"I'm sure she's fine," Dorothy answered. "Or, my mother would have said something."

Parish nodded, twisting one of his blond braids, a habit Beauty had discouraged.

"We could ask at the white farmhouse," Dorothy suggested. "They have a good view up there."

Parish turned toward the house.

They both witnessed a large dark man exit the front door.

"That's Renault," Parish said. Then he let out a loud hoot to get Renault's attention.

They could see Renault jump up in the air, wave both arms at them to come and then disappear in the house.

"Your mother lives there," Dorothy surmised.

Sure enough, the gigantic house belonged to Beauty and Renault. The couple was given the entire tour of the house after official handshakes and hugs were exchanged. Renault's fur-trading profits had provided the funds for the building.

"This place must have a hundred bedrooms," Parish said. "What are you going to do with all this room?"

"It's a stage coach stop for now," Beauty said proudly. "Until my son gets the farm to make a profit and enough grandchildren to fill it."

Dorothy clapped her hands with excitement. "One of the dreams I had in the sweat-lodge in Fort Wayne was a house with lots of doors and children running in and out. If Parish and I remain childless, I could run a school for the children. Father Sebastian will let us borrow books."

* * *

The budding twins, Renault and Susan, safe in Dorothy's very pregnant belly, knew otherwise…at least the childless part. Four children would follow the twins onto God's good earth.

The End

About Rohn Federbush

Rohn Federbush retired as an administrator from the University of Michigan in 1999. She received a Masters of Arts in Creative Writing in 1995 from Eastern Michigan University, where she studied under Janet Kauffman and Larry Smith. In 1998, Vermont College awarded her a summer conference scholarship to work on her novel under Ellen Lesser and Brett Lott. Frederick Busch of Colgate granted a 1997 summer stipend for her ghost-story collection. Michael Joyce of Vassar encouraged earlier writing at Jackson Community College, Jackson, Michigan in 1981. Rohn has completed fourteen novels, with an additional mystery nearly finished, 120 short stories and 150 poems to date.

You can find Rohn on:
Facebook / Twitter / Goodreads /LinkedIn

And on her website:
www.RohnFederbush.com

Made in the USA
Charleston, SC
25 January 2014